Ian dusted off his hands. "You're a rare woman."

Pleasure thrummed through Meredith. "Thank you. That's kind of you to say."

"I'm not just saying it. I'm meaning it." He cast a look around them. "Since I've arrived, I've seen any number of miners tromp over here. You sew and do laundry and write letters for them. Every last one has spoken of marriage to you."

Her jaw dropped.

"Before you think I've eavesdropped, a handful have proposed to you in my presence, and Tucker told me the rest have done likewise. Know this, Meredith Smith: I'm speaking from an earnest heart, not out of flattery in hopes of gaining a wife to wash and mend my clothes."

"Oh." She wasn't sure what more to say.

"I'd best get back to work."

"Me, too." She watched him stride over to the smokehouse, hop down into the hole in the earth he'd been digging, and take up his pickax. *So he's not attracted to me. Ian's the first man I've met in Alaska who appeals to me, and he doesn't even want a wife.*

CATHY MARIE HAKE is a Southern California native who loves her work as a nurse and Lamaze teacher. She and her husband have a daughter, a son, and three dogs, so life is never dull or quiet. Cathy considers herself a sentimental packrat, collecting antiques and Hummel figurines. In spare moments, she reads, bargain hunts, and makes a huge mess with her new hobby of scrapbooking. Cathy@CathyMarieHake.com

Books by Cathy Marie Hake

HEARTSONG PRESENTS

HP370—Twin Victories
HP481—Unexpected Delivery
HP512—Precious Burdens
HP545—Love Is Patient
HP563—Redeemed Hearts
HP583—Ramshackle Rose
HP600—Restoration
HP624—One Chance in a Million
HP648—Last Chance
HP657—Love Worth Finding

HP688—A Handful of Flowers
HP696—Bridal Veil
HP704—No Buttons or Beaux
HP712—Spoke of Love
HP718—In His Will

Don't miss out on any of our super romances. Write to us at the following address for information on our newest releases and club information.

Heartsong Presents Readers' Service
PO Box 721
Uhrichsville, OH 44683

Or visit www.heartsongpresents.com

Golden Dawn

Cathy Marie Hake

Heartsong Presents

This book is dedicated to my dear readers who spend what little leisure time they have with me. Sharing the Lord's goodness and mercy with sisters in Christ is a delight, and I appreciate you!

A note from the Author:
I love to hear from my readers! You may correspond with me by writing:

Cathy Marie Hake
Author Relations
PO Box 721
Uhrichsville, OH 44683

ISBN 978-1-59789-410-4

GOLDEN DAWN

All scripture quotations are taken from the King James Version of the Bible.

All of the characters and events in this book are fictitious. Any resemblance to actual persons, living or dead, or to actual events is purely coincidental.

Our mission is to publish and distribute inspirational products offering exceptional value and biblical encouragement to the masses.

PRINTED IN THE U.S.A.

one

April 1897, Oregon

"Bess and I are ready to go." Ian Rafferty set down the pail from the morning milking and kissed his mother's cheek.

"Not until you eat a sound breakfast." Though Ma's words sounded cheerful, her forced smile and the way she clung to his sleeve warned Ian she'd still not accepted his decision to go to Alaska. For the past three weeks, she'd split her time between helping him supply himself for this trip and begging him not to go.

Bess brayed outside, a sure sign she resented being hitched to the post. As soon as the mule wore a yoke or a pack, she wanted to work.

"Buckwheat pancakes," Ma coaxed. "You'll not be getting those in a good, long while. Sit yourself down."

"Okay, Ma. Just for breakfast."

Da entered the kitchen and sniffed the air. "Braden, if I'm not mistaken, I smell your wife's sugar-cured ham."

Ian's brother nodded. "You do. There's none better than my Maggie's."

The family gathered around the table. Eggs from their henhouse, ham from their hog, and the cream from their cow all testified to God's providence. Da took his place at the head of the table. Instead of folding his calloused hands as he normally did, he reached over and took Ian's and Braden's hands. Braden promptly took Maggie's, and their sister, Fiona, and Mama completed the circle.

"Almighty Father, we give You praise for all You've done on our behalf, for the safety and love and bounty we've enjoyed by Your hand. Now, Father, we ask You to extend those blessings to our Ian as he ventures on in life. Though we'll be parted in body, keep us close in mind and heart we pray, amen."

"Thanks, Da."

Da squeezed Ian's hand. "I have faith God will be with you on your adventure."

Fiona sighed. "I wish I were going."

"You"—Braden waved his fork at their sister—"would gladly go anywhere so long as it was away from here."

"It makes no sense." Ma dabbed at the corners of her eyes with her napkin. "Your da and I risked life and limb coming across the trail so our children would have a better life. There's not a place in the world half as lovely as the farm we've established."

"The Oregon Trail was your adventure," Ian said as he passed the bowl of scrambled eggs. "The Yukon will be mine."

Ma shook her head. "There's no need to go seek your fortune, Ian. Your da and I claimed sufficient land for both of our sons to farm. Fertile land."

"The land's not going anywhere." Ian set down the platter of buckwheat pancakes without taking any. He'd wanted to leave at daybreak just to avoid this unpleasantness. Ever since the day he'd announced his plan to join the Alaska gold rush, Ma had pleaded with him to reconsider. The tears welling in her eyes tore at him.

"I'm a proud man, but I'm not a fool. If I get up there and things are truly as miserable as you believe, I'll come home and admit I chased a rainbow." He softened his voice. "Now that I've given that pledge, let's not waste our last hour together with harsh words."

Ian looked across the table at his older brother. Braden plowed through life with unshakable confidence. He'd loved their farm and grown up looking forward to working the acreage, marrying his childhood sweetheart, and rearing their children here. *He's already done the first two, and a more content man I'll ne'er meet. How can it be that he's so stable and I'm so restless?*

Braden cleared his throat. "Maggie and I—we thought this would be a grand time to lighten your hearts by telling you all that we're going to have a babe."

Maggie patted Ma's hand. "Braden's already decided this will be a son, and he's planned on twelve more babes—a baker's dozen, he calls it. I'll be grateful for your help."

Ma promptly swiped the coffee mug from Maggie and shoved a glass of milk in front of her. "You need to drink plenty of milk. Hedda Libman told me while I carried Braden 'tis an old wives' tale that a woman loses a tooth for each child. All she has to do is drink a quart of milk a day."

Da chuckled. "Aye, 'twas sound advice. Look at your beautiful smile."

Ian rapidly wolfed down his food in hopes that the conversation would last long enough to let him slip away. Bess brayed again, and he shot to his feet. "Ma, those pancakes were the best ever. Maggie, same with your ham. Sis, keep on with your studies. Smart as you are, someday you might be a schoolmarm yourself."

Fiona scowled. "Not me. I'm going to become a doctor."

Da laughed aloud. "A few years back, you planned to become a librarian. Before that, you wanted to be a famous painter."

"Those were childish dreams." Fiona's chin lifted in a stubborn tilt. "I'm of an age to plan my future."

"And 'tis time I set out to meet my future." Ian bent to press a kiss on Ma's pale cheek. "I'll be careful."

He hugged his sister and whispered, " 'Tis no shame to dream."

"It's not just a dream, Ian," she whispered back.

He straightened and turned to Maggie. "I remember you bringing your doll to church because you wanted her to learn about Jesus. With all that practicing, you'll be a fine mother."

Maggie blushed and murmured something that got lost in Braden's proud, "I'll watch out for her."

"You do that." Ian unashamedly embraced his older brother.

Braden growled, "Go and enjoy yourself. Don't be sheepish in the least if you decide to come back to us. You're no prodigal, but even if you were, Da would have to race me to the barn to kill the fatted calf."

Ian chuckled. "If you'd seen the supplies I have waiting in town to take, you'd think I'd already killed that calf! Ma thought up more stuff for me to take than you can shake a stick at."

"You'll be glad to have it," Ma predicted.

Da promised to take good care of things.

With a heavily laden mule, a Bible, and high hopes, Ian set out on his adventure.

❧

Goose Chase, Alaska

Wind whipped the air, and chunks of ice cracked and knocked together as the river began to thaw. Meredith Smith turned her face to the weak spring sun and relished the small bit of light and warmth it yielded. After a long, dark winter, even the slightest ribbon of light lifted her spirits.

Tucker straightened from the bank of the river and lifted his net. "Sis! How's this?"

Tilting her head to the side, she studied the fish. "If it were any bigger, he'd be eating us for dinner!" Her twin grinned, and Meredith's heart soared. Tucker seldom smiled. She understood why, but that made these rare moments all the sweeter.

"Bring me a bucket. I'm going to see if I can't catch more."

Meredith lugged a wooden bucket to him. "If the others are anywhere near that big, the only thing that'll hold them is a bathtub."

"It'll be good to have fresh meat." Tucker dumped the trout into the tub and turned back to try to net more. A craggy formation of rocks stuck out into the river from their claim; then the river suddenly widened from that point. The water continued to rush past, but some swirled into the wider space in an eddy in which fish sometimes took refuge. When Tucker spotted that land feature, it cinched this as the land he chose for their claim.

Meredith watched the fish thrash in the confines of the bucket. "You've caught us a tasty lunch."

"Wish we had some cornmeal. Then he'd taste better when you fry him."

"I might be able to find some herbs. I'm starting to see a few sprouts coming up here and there."

"Don't try anything you're not sure of." He leaned forward and squinted at the water.

Meredith didn't reply. She and Tucker saw life from opposite perspectives: he saw the pitfalls, while she looked for the possibilities. Long ago, he hadn't been that way. Ever since the debacle, Tucker's view of life had changed. She'd learned to allow her brother his mutterings and weigh whether they bore consideration or were merely manifestations of the burdens he shouldered.

"Sis?"

Meredith turned around. "Yes?"

Tucker grimaced. "I know we need to buy supplies, but

I owe plenty of folks money. Make a list of the absolute essentials, and we'll talk it over later."

"Are we going to town tomorrow?"

"I haven't decided. I don't want to leave you here, but taking you is dangerous."

"Dangerous?" Meredith laughed. "We made it through a winter in Alaska. We're tough enough to survive a trip to town."

"I knew it. I knew you'd grow to hate this isolation. You—"

"Tucker, if you dare say anything about me leaving here and going to Uncle Darian, I'm going to push you in the river. Never once—not a single time—have I regretted coming here with you. We're family, and we belong together. No matter where I live, there'll always be challenges. In Texas, it was the heat and lack of water. Before that, it was the tornadoes in Kansas."

"Last time, you said it was the thunderstorms and flash floods," he grumbled.

"See? That just bolsters my argument. I'm going to make that list of essentials, and at the very top of it, I'm going to write 'handcuffs.'" Her brother gave her a startled look. Meredith shook her finger at him. "God linked us together the day He created us as twins. If locking us together is the only way I can keep you from trying to send me away, I'll do it."

"It's not right—"

"I agree." Meredith knew she'd abandoned her manners by interrupting him, but too much hung in the balance. "It's not right for you to try to send me off to Uncle Darian."

"He's family."

"Not as close as you are." She folded her arms across her chest. "I'm winning this argument. You know I am. You haven't come up with a single valid point, and we've gone round and round about it for more than a year."

"You're stubborn as a mule."

Meredith closed the distance between them. She hugged her brother. "I love you, too."

"You ought to." He tugged her to the side. "I just caught another fish."

They'd survived the winter on smoked fish, beans, and corn mush. To be sure, Tucker also supplemented their diet with snow hare he snared and meat for which he bartered.

"With the river thawing, this is going to be a good fishing day. I'll fill this bucket with water, and we can keep a few alive in the cabin so they'll be fresh the next couple of days."

"Wonderful!" She thought for a moment. They'd made it through the winter only with very careful planning and God's providence. The number of meals she had sufficient supplies left to make could be counted on one hand. "I'll gather wood, and we can smoke some fish, too."

"I don't want you wandering off."

"I'll stay close by." Glancing at the empty claim beside theirs, she added, "I wonder if Percy made it to town."

"Based on pure orneriness, I'd say he did." Tucker jerked up on the net and growled when he saw he'd caught nothing.

"Are you referring to his orneriness or yours?"

Tucker gave Meredith his full attention. "You're full of sass today."

"And you're grumpy. I guess we deserve one another." She laughed as she walked away.

A stand of trees stood a ways back from their tiny cabin. As the snows began to melt, branches that had fallen were revealed. Meredith dragged back a spruce limb. It sledded along the icy ground, making the task manageable. Tucker would take an ax to it later. Gathering fuel was essential both for cooking and for heat. Especially for heat.

Meredith pulled her rust-colored woolen cloak more tightly

about herself. Though the calendar indicated spring had arrived, cold was a constant companion.

Percy, their neighbor, had arrived on the same ship she and Tucker had traveled on. They'd taken neighboring claims. By midwinter, Percy had declared that if he survived the cold, he'd return home and live out his days in the blessed warmth of California.

After dragging over two more branches, Meredith sat down and started composing a list of essentials. She did so on a slate. Paper was too costly up here. More important, she could erase items and script in some other much-needed item without Tucker being any the wiser. Eager to enjoy the sunlight, she sat on a rock and leaned against the cabin wall.

"Coffee," she wrote. They'd run out of coffee halfway through the winter. As much as her brother loved coffee, that counted as a severe hardship. Had just she and Tucker been drinking it, they would have been sufficiently supplied, but men dropped by a lot. Since most of them arrived in this icy frontier alone, they often came over with mending or laundry or questions about cooking. Hospitality prompted Meredith to offer them coffee, but survival forced her not to feed them.

An odd economy developed. Men who sought her assistance soon brought firewood or meat from game they'd shot. Twice, she'd earned enough coffee to make a pot. Just the memory of the taste and aroma of coffee made her mouth water. Oh, and the blessed heat each swallow imparted. Certainly, coffee rated as an essential.

Beans. Rice. Cornmeal. Oatmeal. Salt. Lard. Meredith paused and stared at the list. Flour and sugar would be wonderful, but they'd make do without those luxuries. She didn't want to write down anything for Tucker to eliminate. He'd feel bad if he denied her a single thing.

One item she craved above all else, but she didn't add it to the list. They'd done fairly well with a damaged one this past year. Tucker wanted a decent one just as badly as she did. If she wrote it on the list, it would only cause him needless anguish. Maybe next year they could splurge. Right now, she needed to be sure they wouldn't starve.

"Be sure to put down thread and needles and some buttons," Tucker ordered as he walked up.

"Okay." She bowed her head over the slate.

"Your sewing kept us from starving this winter." He set down the bucket.

"My sewing was responsible for us running out of coffee." She leaned sideways and peered at the fish. "That's a feast for fifteen in there!"

"Four at the most." Though her brother muttered the response, Meredith knew Tucker was proud of what he'd caught. "Why don't you fetch the twine? I'll start a fire, and we can string these up and smoke 'em. Whilst they smoke, I'll catch more."

The fish milled in the bucket, and Meredith gave her brother a delighted look. "You caught a Dolly Varden!"

"It took you long enough to notice." His gruff tone didn't begin to hide his pleasure.

"I'm not smoking it; I'm fixing it for dinner."

He grunted and turned back toward the river.

"Don't you dare pretend that you're slaving away. I know good and well how much you love going fishing."

He shouted over his shoulder, "I deserve this. No doubt, to-morrow you'll pester me into hoeing a patch for your garden."

"I always said you were smart." Meredith looked to the side of their tiny cabin and imagined how wonderful it would be to coax something other than gold from the ground.

❧

Mud sucked at Ian's boots. He'd tied them as tight as they'd allow, but the mud still tried its hardest to rob him of his footwear. Bess trudged along, patiently bearing the packs on her back and the seven-and-a-half-foot sled she pulled. Sure-footed as ever, she didn't seem to mind the bone-chilling cold. Good thing, that. When his mule decided she was too thirsty or tired, she exhibited the famed stubbornness of her kind.

Ian readjusted the straps of the pack on his own back. Despite the cold, excitement pulsed through his veins. Every curve he rounded, every step he took, seemed to feed his sense of adventure. After days on the boat to come up here, he'd gotten his fill of being stuck in close quarters with greedy men. Instead of taking the White Trail or traversing the Chilkoot Pass, he'd determined to go elsewhere. Goose Chase wasn't even on the map, but he'd overheard a few men in Skaguay talking about the tiny town. Taking that as a cue from the Lord, Ian went to Goose Chase.

Everything fell into place. Upon reaching Goose Chase, he met a prospector. Mr. Percy willingly exchanged his claim's deed for ship fare to return to Washington. The ticket cost a pittance—ships emptied of their stampeders gladly booked passage to Seattle at greatly reduced rates just so they'd earn a little rather than none at all.

Then, too, the snowmelt hadn't yet hit the point where the path would turn into an endless mud bog. Bess didn't like mud puddles, and they slowed down her pulling. Enough snow and ice covered the ground to let the sled skim across the surface.

Well, most of the time it did, Ian thought as he struggled to yank his right foot free from a sucking, muddy morass. He straightened up just in time to spy a hawk floating on the currents of the icy north wind.

"Lord, 'tis a majestic place You created here. I can feel it in my bones—'tis where You'd have me be." Ian consulted his map again. "Not far now, Bess. We'll be getting there."

A few minutes later, something struck his shoulder. Ian wheeled around.

"Git offa my land!" A haggard, hairy man stood several feet away. Even from a distance and despite the stranger's unkempt mustache, Ian could see his sneer.

"Just passin' through."

"No, you ain't." The man's eyes narrowed. He bounced his hand up and down, giving Ian a glimpse of the rock he held as a weapon. "Not 'less you brung vittles."

"You're hungry?"

An ugly laugh filled the air. "Boy, you're dumb as a stump. Ain't nobody up here who ain't had his belly growlin' worse'n a grizzly."

From his reading, Ian knew the winters would be horrendous, but he also knew game abounded. He frowned. "Is the hunting hereabouts bad?"

"You gonna gimme grub, or are you gonna turn tail and get offa my claim?"

"A hungry man oughtn't be turned away." Ma's words echoed in his mind. Ma and Da sometimes spoke of how carefully they had to ration food while traversing the Oregon Trail.

Da's advice followed just as swiftly. *"Don't give away more than you can safely afford."*

"I can spare a wee bit."

The man drew closer. "A lot. I wanna lot."

Christian charity prompted Ian to share; prudence demanded that he make sure he kept enough to supply his own needs for a long while. "Here." He pulled the sandwich he'd bought in town from inside a burlap bag. That sandwich cost the exorbitant price of two dollars.

"That's a start. What else you gonna gimme?"

"This and my thanks. If that's not enough, I'll walk the

border of your claim and carry on."

The man grunted, swiped the sandwich, and lumbered off.

By the time Ian made his way around the last bend in the river before nearing his new claim, he'd met two more surly miners. *Whate'er I endure here, Lord, help me stay civil to my fellow man. And, Lord? If You're of a mind, I'd appreciate a good neighbor.*

The next instant, a gunshot tore the air.

two

"Hey!"

"Next shot won't be a warning." Though no one was visible, the voice came from a stand of trees.

"Mr. Abrams?" an unmistakably feminine voice called from across the river. "Are you all right?"

Ian watched in utter amazement as a woman in a rust-colored cape came into view. What was a woman doing out here in the bitterly cold wilds? He immediately whisked off his hat. "Ma'am."

"Mr. Abrams?" she repeated.

"Got me a claim jumper."

Ian heaved a sigh. "I've a claim of my own. I don't want yours."

"You don't want mine?" Mr. Abrams finally stepped into view. "Well, how do you like that? Meredith, this whipper-snapper is insulting my claim!"

"I'm sure it's a grand claim." Ian nodded to emphasize his point.

"Indeed, it is. A very fine claim," the woman tacked on.

"But I'm eager to set to work my own stake." Ian reached into his coat pocket and produced his map. "And I ought to reach it as soon as I cross the river here."

"Did you buy Percy's claim?"

"That I did." Ian squared his shoulders. "Word in Skaguay was that the Chilkoot Pass is nigh unto impassable, but folks are clamoring about the benefits of going that direction any-how. By now, most of the decent claims have to be gone.

I reckoned that heading off in a different direction made sense."

A man joined the woman, and it didn't escape Ian's notice that he held a rifle. She smiled up at her man. Gently pushing the butt of the rifle toward the ground, she said, "This gentleman is our new neighbor."

"Ian Rafferty."

The man studied him for a moment, then rasped, "Tucker and Meredith Smith." It didn't escape Ian's notice that Tucker Smith still kept a tight grip on his weapon.

"Pleased to make your acquaintance." Cold as it was, Ian longed to slap his hat back on, but that would be rude. He turned a shade to his left. "And I gather you're Mr. Abrams."

Mr. Abrams kicked the muddy sled. "You might make it 'cross, but ain't no way to get your b'longings over."

The woman looked at the chunks of ice bobbing on the rough current. "I'm sure the gentleman must have a plan, Mr. Abrams." She turned her gaze onto Ian.

"Indeed, I do."

"Tucker and I are willing to help."

Tucker's head dipped once in curt agreement.

"Name him a steep price," Abrams advised. "He's got plenty."

"I will not!" Tucker boomed in outrage. He turned his attention on Ian. "We offered our help, and it's yours. What's your plan?"

During his trek, Ian had considered this eventuality and formulated a plan. "I've a ball of twine—"

Abrams hooted with laughter.

Ian pretended the miner hadn't made a sound. "I'll tie one end to an arrow and shoot it into that pine. Once 'tis on your side, if you can pull the twine, I'll tie a sturdy rope to the end. Once we've hitched the line betwixt trees, I can ferry parcels across."

"No use you doing that much work—especially with the river so mean right now." Tucker shook his head. "We can each have a line and stay on opposite sides. It'll be safer and quicker."

"That's a generous offer. I've a pair of pulleys. They'll make things glide more smoothly."

"Now just you hold on a minute." Mr. Abrams scowled. "You're supposing I'll allow you to use one of my trees."

Lord, give me patience. This old coot's quibbling over something that petty?

"Smith might be willing to help you outta Christian charity, but I'm not." Abrams smacked himself in the chest. "Bible-thumpin' folks can do what they please, but charity begins at home, and you're standin' on my property."

Ian set aside his irritation over the man's greed as his heart jumped at how quickly the Lord had answered his prayers to have Christian neighbors.

"Mr. Abrams," the woman called in a sweet voice, "I'm sure you'll be willing to help out while I prepare supper. Then we can all break bread together to welcome Mr. Rafferty properly."

Abrams's eyes lit up. "You got bread? Real flour-built bread?"

Even from across the water, Ian watched as her features pulled, then quickly resumed a strained smile. *She's out of flour.* He blurted out, "The first thing I'll send over is flour. It's only right that I contribute something to the meal."

"Oh, that would be wonderful!" The joy in her voice was unmistakable.

"I hope it's not too much trouble for you to bake it."

"Not at all!" Suddenly, her beaming smile faded. "Oh. Well, I mean, I have soda. I can bake biscuits. We ran out of flour awhile ago, so I've lost my starter."

"I've a small packet of sourdough starter I bought from an

old woman in Skaguay. That and a few cakes of Fleischmann's yeast." *For all of her upset o'er me leaving, Ma gave me fine directions on the essentials. I'd have never thought of starter.*

Mrs. Smith pressed a hand to her bosom and said in a shaky voice, "You have starter?"

The last thing he wanted to do was set a woman to tears. Ian scuffed a small pebble with the toe of his boot and wondered what else they'd run out of. Whatever it was, he'd do his best to share. They'd already offered their friendship and help. He could do no less. "I'd take it as a favor if you'd use the starter I brought and freshen it. Left to myself, I'm afraid I'd not bake for another few days and have it go bad."

Tucker said something to her, and she nodded before walking off.

"We ain't got all day." Abrams motioned at Ian. "Get busy." As soon as Ian pulled out his bow, the crusty man gave it a dubious look. "Sure you can hit the broad side of a barn with that?"

"I'll be hitting that spot where the bark's scraped off of the pine," Ian called out to Tucker. A moment later, the arrow cut the air and landed precisely where he'd said it would.

Tucker whistled. "Impressive."

"I'd be more impressed if he'd hit something I could eat." Abrams watched as Ian tied his end of the twine to a rope. Tucker pulled the twine until the rope spanned the river. Once Tucker secured it to the pine, Abrams started dragging the other end toward a fat old red alder. "Got them pulleys, or are they stuck somewhere in that big mess of junk you hauled up here?"

"Here they are." Ian pulled them from the burlap bag he'd tied with string. He felt every bit as eager to get to his claim as Abrams was to eat.

Tucker stood with his feet braced apart and rested his

hand on his hips. "Don't give in to the temptation to go fast and heavy on the loads. Make them light and well balanced. Better that you take time and save it all than go quick and drop something in the drink. You can't afford to lose anything up here."

It took just slightly under four hours to set up the rig and transfer his possessions over the tumultuous water. As the last load went across, Abrams kicked the sled. "What're you gonna do with this now?"

"Taking it over." Ian had plans for every part of that sled.

Abrams scowled at him. "You tetched in the head?"

"Not that I know." Ian chuckled. "But if I were, I suppose I'd be the last to know."

"Humph."

Bess balked at crossing the river, but she finally did so. She twitched, shook, and brayed once she hit land. Tucker picked up what looked to be a burlap sack and started to dry her off a bit.

Lord, You exceeded my very thoughts and wishes with the Tuckers for my neighbors. They're God-fearing, helpful, and even show consideration to a beast. Thank You for settling me next to them.

Ian held fast to the rope and swung his feet up. Mud splattered off his boots as he crossed his ankles over the rope. Pulling himself from one side of the river to the other didn't strain him in the least. If anything, each moment managed to invigorate him further. As soon as he hit ground, he went over to assume Bess's care.

"She's fine." Tucker ruffled the mule's coarse mane. She wandered off and cropped at some fresh grass.

"Thanks for seeing to her." Ian took out his bandanna and dipped it in the water. As he started to wash the grime from his hands and face, he called out, "Come on over, Mr. Abrams. The rope's sturdy."

Abrams coughed and spat. "I'm too old for that nonsense."

"Oh, but supper will be ready in a jiffy," Mrs. Smith called to him. "I set a place for you."

"Can't disappoint the lady." Abrams swung up on the rope and shimmied over with more dexterity than Ian had expected. The old man dropped down next to Tucker Smith. "Been so long since I had me some bread, I woulda swum over here to have a taste."

"You can't swim," Tucker said.

"Woulda lernt how." Abrams marched toward the cabin.

Until that moment, Ian hadn't paid much attention to the small building. Percy said he'd erected a shelter on the claim. Though small, it looked sturdy enough. If anything, the nine-by-ten-foot log cabin would be generous for a man on his own. *A bigger place would require more wood to heat. This is perfect for me.*

He and Tucker followed close behind the old man. "Once we eat and Abrams makes it back to his claim, I'll help you use the rope to hang your provender."

Ian gave Tucker a surprised look. "I appreciate the offer, but it hardly seems necessary."

"Bears and raccoons are active. Most of this could be gone in a day."

Ian shrugged. "The cabin looks quite sturdy."

Confusion plowed lines on Smith's forehead. "You want me to store your goods?"

"Dinner's going to get cold," the woman called to them from the door.

At that moment, Ian realized this was her home, not his. "My apologies. I mistook your cabin for mine."

Tucker's brows shot upward. "What cabin?"

"Hooo-ooo-ey!" Abrams wheeled around and laughed so hard, he started coughing. "Percy snookered you!"

Dread filled Ian. "He swore he'd constructed a shelter."

"He did." Abrams pointed to a half-hidden jumble of logs. "He just didn't tell you what kind."

When he stared at the ramshackle lean-to, Ian questioned the sanity of his plan for the first time.

three

"Tucker caught an abundance of fish today."

"I brung my appetite with me. I could eat the legs off a runnin' skunk." Abrams smacked Ian on the shoulder. "Betcha you're starvin' after walking all this way."

Until he'd seen the lean-to, Ian had felt ravenous. But his appetite had disappeared. Just before he said so, he looked at Mrs. Smith. *Miss Smith*, he thought as he got a closer look at her abundant brown hair and warm hazel eyes. Her features were finer and softer than Tucker's, but there could be no mistaking the truth. They weren't man and wife—they were brother and sister.

"Are you hungry, Mr. Rafferty?" Her glance darted to the lean-to and back.

Ian suddenly remembered his manners and whisked off his hat. He didn't want to lie, so he settled on the only truth he could muster. "Something smells wonderful, ma'am."

"It's your bread." She inhaled deeply. "In the Bible, there's talk of incense burning before the Lord. I don't know about all the sweet-smelling things they used, but I won't be disappointed if heaven smells like fresh, hot bread."

"If that was true, I might could think 'bout mendin' my ways and getting churchified." Mr. Abrams plowed on into the cabin.

Accustomed to stomping the field soil from his shoes and wiping his feet on the veranda mat, Ian noticed the Smiths had no such mat. His next realization was that the cabin had a dirt floor. Nonetheless, he stomped his feet and did his best

24

to knock off the worst of the dried crumbles.

"No need for that," Miss Smith murmured.

"I'd beg to disagree. Your floor is hard packed; the soil on my boots would scatter all over and make a mess." He flashed her a wry smile. "Besides, my ma would wallop me if she ever heard I tracked dirt into anyone's house."

Miss Smith laughed.

A table made of raw-cut timber completely filled the space between a pair of beds. Packing crates formed a crude storage area along the far wall on each side of a stone fireplace. Most of the dishes sat on the table; an appalling lack of food on the shelves stunned Ian. *And still, they invited me to supper.*

"You men can sit on that side." Tucker waved at one of the beds. He sat next to his sister on the other.

"How lovely to have you gentlemen join us." Miss Smith's hazel eyes sparkled with delight.

She's living on the edge of hunger, yet she's glad to share. Ian smiled at her. "Honored to be invited, ma'am. It's generous of you."

"Yeah." Abrams nodded as he swiped the biggest slice of bread and stuffed half of it in his mouth.

"In our home, we ask a blessing before each meal." Tucker folded his hands.

Abrams crammed the rest of the bread in his mouth and bowed his head. The second Tucker's prayer ended, Abrams grabbed for another slice of bread and squinted at Tucker. "Dunno much about all that God stuff, but didn't you forget one of your lines? The one 'bout daily bread?"

"That's the Lord's Prayer." Tucker lifted the platter of fish and started to pass it to Ian.

Ian tilted his head toward Miss Smith. "Ladies first."

Tucker's brow rose, but he held the platter so his sister could serve herself.

Abrams took a gigantic bite of the bread and spoke with his mouth full. "Ain't all the prayers His?"

Miss Smith served her brother first, then herself. "All of our prayers are said to the Lord, but Jesus taught the disciples one as an example of how to pray. We call that the Lord's Prayer."

"Humph. Just as well." The old man took the platter and speared the largest fish with his fork. As he lifted, the fish flaked apart and half flopped back onto the platter. He scraped the fish directly from the platter onto his plate and plunked the platter down without offering it to Ian. "I recollect there's another part of that prayer that don't settle with me. I ain't no trespasser, and I ain't a-gonna forgive nobody else for trespassing on my claim."

"Jesus forgives all of us if we ask Him to. Christians want to be like Him, so we try to forgive others." Miss Smith deftly lifted Abrams's mug and pressed it into his hand as he reached for a third slice of bread.

Tucker pushed the bread toward Ian. Tucker's eyes gave a silent bid for him to hurry and claim his fair share.

Ian took a slice and immediately gave the plate to Tucker. "After you and Miss Smith help yourselves, perhaps you could set this behind you."

"No reason to do that," Abrams roared with outrage.

"Of course there is. I'm clumsy." Ian pointed at the serving platter that lay off center in the middle of the tiny table. "I aim to scoot that closer, or I'm going to drop fish on the table and make a mess." He proceeded to pull the entrée over and serve himself.

"As I said"—Tucker cleared his throat—"bears can be a problem around here."

Ian grimaced. "Then how did Percy live in a lean-to?"

"Stink." Abrams bobbed his head knowingly. "He stunk so bad, bears like to thought he was a skunk."

Miss Smith coughed. *Is she really choking, or is she trying to hide laughter?*

"Tucker, whap her on the back a few times. Something's going down the wrong pipe." Abrams waggled his fork in the air. "Yep. Stink's what kept the bears from Percy."

Miss Smith's cough turned to a splutter. If Mr. Abrams had bathed even once in the past six months, Ian would have been amazed. Out in the open, his smell hadn't been quite so overpowering, but in the close confines of the cabin, Abrams's stench grew stronger by the second. Opening the one tiny window wouldn't begin to help.

"Miss Smith"—Ian looked across the table at her—"do you need some fresh air?"

Tucker grabbed his plate and hers as he shot to his feet. "Good of you to understand, Rafferty. Come, Sis. We'll all go on outside to finish supper. After the long winter, it's best you get as much light and fresh air as you can."

"Since you insist." She rose with alacrity.

"Go on ahead." Abrams sounded downright jolly. "I'll get the bread."

"I'll tend to that." Ian smiled. "Since her brother's hands are full, I'll help the lady with her cape."

Miss Smith nodded. "Then I'll carry the bread."

Abrams made a disgruntled sound and trundled outside.

Ian took Miss Smith's cape from the peg by the door. "I hope you'll leave some of the loaf in here so you can have it tomorrow morning."

"You won't mind?"

"Why would I?" He slid the russet wool over her shoulders. "You baked it."

"But it's your flour." She said that last word almost reverently.

"No, it wasn't." He couldn't help himself. He moved her thick, glossy brown braid. It felt every bit as soft as it looked.

"Just as your brother shared the fish he caught and you shared your labor, I shared the flour."

"You bringin' that bread out here?" Abrams hollered.

Ian chuckled. "Now set aside some for yourselves before that ornery old man eats it all."

ۂ

Meredith sat outside by the fire. Smoke filtered up from it and through the fish Tucker had strung earlier in the day. That bounty, alone, already caused her to praise God for His provision today. The bread just proved how generous the Lord continued to be toward her and Tucker.

"You gonna eat that bread, or are you just gonna stare at it?"

"Of course she's going to eat it," Tucker half growled.

Mr. Abrams stuck out his lower lip like a pouting toddler. "No need to get touchy. Just didn't want good food to go to waste."

"It was good food." Mr. Rafferty set his plate down on the rock beside him and nodded at her. "Miss Smith, you're a grand cook." After she murmured her thanks, Mr. Rafferty gestured toward the line of fish. "And, Tucker, you're quite the fisherman. That's an impressive day's catch. I know for certain I'll never come close to a haul like that."

Though she appreciated the compliment Mr. Rafferty paid to her cooking, Meredith especially appreciated how he praised her brother. Tucker enjoyed fishing and was proud of having provided well for their meal. Having someone recognize his contribution—that mattered.

"I'm a miserable fisherman," Mr. Rafferty continued. "But I do like to hunt. Once I erect a cabin, I'm planning to build a smokehouse."

"You handled that bow well today." Tucker skidded the last bite of his bread over his plate, gathering the last little flakes of fish. "Even so, I'm glad to see you brought a firearm."

"I read a fair bit when I decided to come north. Judging from the landscape and region, I'm hoping to get grouse, pheasant, and rabbit. My bow will serve me well with those wee creatures. As for my rifle—one good-sized mountain sheep or caribou would certainly provide endless meals."

"No caribou here. No deer, either." Abrams burped loudly. "You'd be smart to pan gold and pay for more supplies to see you through the winter. That canvas you brought— just double it over the lean-to, and you'll be snug enough. You don't have time to waste building a cabin, let alone a smokehouse. That plan's pure foolishness."

Mr. Rafferty stared at the fire. Most men would have been insulted, but he didn't react. After a moment's silence, he asked, "Are you folks familiar with a man by the name of Wily?"

"Yes," Meredith said.

"Who isn't?" Abrams scowled. "Worthless waste of a man."

"Wily's a good man," Tucker disagreed. "Salt of the earth."

"Salt?" Abrams spat off to the side. "If that's what you want, he'll bring it. Won't deliver what's important, though."

Tucker shrugged. "A man has the right to run his own business. Wily's reliable. If he agrees to ferry someone or deliver something, his word is his bond."

Relief radiated from their new neighbor. "Percy introduced me to him. After I learned that Percy had hedged regarding the shelter, I wondered if he and Wily were in cahoots. Wily's to bring the remainder of my possessions in his boat."

"You've got more stuff a-comin'?" Abrams leaned forward. "Like what?"

"Necessities."

Abrams slapped his knee. "Now that was downright smart of you. Wily wouldn't pry. You said necessities, and he don't think the way you and me do. He won't guess what you got. I'm your neighbor. When—"

"If you're thinking I have spirits or tobacco coming, you're mistaken. Neither appeals to me, and they're certainly not essential."

While Abrams moaned and groaned, Tucker rose. "Speaking of necessities, we'd better string up the supplies you brought before we lose our light."

"Hold on a second." Abrams looked like a drowning man grasping for even the smallest twig. "Ain't you gonna brew us up some coffee now, Meredith? You always make coffee when you got guests."

"Which is why we ran out." Tucker locked eyes with Mr. Rafferty. "Learn from our mistake. There'll be no coffee tonight."

"Now why'd you hafta go ruin it?" Abrams trundled toward the rope. "No use me stickin' round here any longer. Time's better spent workin' my claim." Once he crabbed his way across the river, the old man untied the rope from his tree. The cold air carried his dark mutterings.

As Mr. Rafferty pulled the rope over to his claim, Meredith gathered the dishes. The men sorted the supplies, and Meredith forced herself to wash the dishes. She oughtn't bustle over and stick her nose in the new neighbor's business. Though he seemed friendly enough, she didn't want him to feel as if they were trying to get on his good side so he'd give them food.

It didn't take them long to suspend the food from a tree. Rafferty accompanied Tucker back to their fire. "Sis, Mr. Rafferty's asked to sleep by the fire here tonight. He'll add logs so the fish'll smoke."

"Will you be warm enough?" As soon as she blurted out the question, Meredith regretted her haste. They didn't have blankets to spare.

" 'Tis kind of you to ask, but I've warm blankets aplenty."

He set down the bundle he'd carried in his left arm and carefully propped his rifle so it pointed away from the cabin.

The fire flickered again, and Meredith's breath caught. Atop his dark wool blanket rested a brown leather book. "Is that a Bible?"

"It is." He smiled. "It's a blessing to know I have believers for my new neighbors."

"Could you. . .would you. . ." Tears filled her eyes.

Tucker wrapped an arm around her shoulders and pulled her close. "Our Bible got wet. We tried to dry it, but pages started to mold. I cut the spine and salvaged half of it. I think my sister is asking if you'd mind reading something aloud."

"Not at all." He picked up the Bible and held it out to her. "Why don't you choose what you'd like? Tucker, you can read it to us."

She relished the weight of the whole Bible. How could something that felt so heavy make her heart feel so light?

"What would you like, Sis?"

A psalm? A passage of Exodus where the children of God were in the wilderness? Job, who suffered the unthinkable and turned to praise God? The choice overwhelmed her. "Anything. Anything at all."

Tucker let out a low, long rumble of laughter.

In that moment, Meredith knew she'd never forget this moment or the neighbor God sent to make it happen. Mr. Rafferty hadn't brought bread alone. He'd brought the Word of God, and he'd done the impossible. He'd broken a year and a half's bleakness by making her brother laugh.

four

Ian squatted by the fire and moved the speckled enamelware coffeepot. The brew would feel good going down after the cold night. Odd, how yesterday had been so bitterly cold, yet a warm wind replaced the frigid gusts today. All around him, patches of snow melted away, and the river widened as the frozen edges thawed.

Through the night and even now, Ian kept the fire low—just enough to keep a nice, steady stream of blue smoke wending up to the fish.

The cabin door opened. "Good morning!" Miss Smith sounded as cheery as a lark.

"Morning." Her brother sounded downright surly.

"Top o' the mornin' to you both." Ian grinned. He'd grown up with his father saying that phrase, and somehow it seemed right to use it now, himself.

Tucker's eyes widened. "Is that coffee?"

"It is. You declared there'd be no coffee last night. I didn't want to make a liar of you, so I waited 'til this morning to brew a pot. It should be ready any minute now. Go get your mugs."

"You're not obliged to share," Miss Smith murmured.

"I'm happy to."

Tucker cleared his throat. "I'm a proud man. I'm glad you offered, because I might have sunk to begging for a sip if you hadn't."

Ian finally stood. "If my sister were here, you might have to do just that. Fiona's been known to drink an entire pot of coffee all on her own before breakfast ever reached the table."

"Smart gal." Tucker nodded his approval.

"You don't know just how smart she is." Ian stretched out the words with relish. "Whilst I gathered my supplies, she insisted upon me bringing another can of Arbuckle's. Said it would keep me warm in the dead of winter."

"Arbuckle's," Tucker groaned.

"His favorite." Miss Smith laughed. "I'll go fetch the mugs."

"Bowls and spoons, too," Ian called out to her. "I'm not much of a cook, but oatmeal doesn't take much attention."

While she disappeared into the cabin, Tucker shifted his weight and studied the toes of his boots. "We're not in a position to return your—"

"Seasoned. That's what they called it." Ian squatted, stirred the oatmeal, and repeated, "Seasoned. When the Colonists first came to the New World, someone who made it a whole year was called 'seasoned.' That's what you are. There's plenty I don't know. If I ply you with coffee, I reckon it won't seem so much like I'm pestering you with my questions."

Miss Smith reappeared. They said grace and breakfasted outside. Scents of smoke, pine, coffee, and fish mingled in the air. Casual conversation flowed. Miss Smith reached out and touched one of the fish that hung over the low fire. "In another hour or so, I'll be able to store those away."

"I'll catch more today."

She shook her finger at her brother. "Not until you start my gardening plot. You promised you'd hoe me one as soon as we got our first chinook."

"*Chinook* is an unseasonably warm wind," Tucker explained. He turned back to his sister. "The growing season's not long enough to make it worth your while."

Unable to bear the disappointment flickering across her face, Ian spoke up. "I brought seeds, myself."

Miss Smith's jaw dropped. "You did?"

Tucker gave him a wary look. "Most men wouldn't bother. First and only thing they care about is getting gold."

"I'm not like most men." Ian lifted the coffeepot and poured the last of its contents into Tucker's cup. "Getting the gold is only part of my plan. But I came to succeed, not to plunder the land and run off. Having a solid roof over my head and food for my table—that will allow me to remain put and be a success in the long haul."

Tucker took a sip of coffee and said nothing.

"You folks have been more than kind, but I don't want to test your hospitality by making a mistake again about the property line. What landmarks did you and Percy establish?"

"The pile of rocks right there"—Tucker nodded toward the riverbank, then tilted his head in the opposite direction—"to the red alders back there."

"Mr. Clemment holds the land on your opposite side." Miss Smith stared into her mug. "There's a bramble between your properties, and you're best to leave it alone. He means no one any harm. He's rather. . .eccentric."

"I'll keep that in mind." Ian surveyed the area and thought aloud. "There's enough for my mule to forage for a while, but I won't be able to keep her in feed all winter long. For a while, she'll be useful, though. I can hitch her to pull the logs for my cabin. Until I fell the trees, she's got nothing to do. Would you like to use her to start your garden?"

"Nice offer." Tucker sounded like a man doomed to a tedious chore. "But we don't have a plow."

"Neither do I, but I have a plan."

About an hour later, Tucker looked over the odd apparatus they'd put together. "You know, this thing just might work, after all."

They'd taken the skids from the sled Bess had pulled the supplies on and used them along with a spade, a plank, wires, and leather straps to create a plow. "It's a sorry-looking oddity, but it'll work." Ian jostled it. "Pretty sturdy, all things considered. We'll hitch it up to Bess, and you can start that garden for your sister."

"Nope." Tucker rested his hands on his hips. "You plow both gardens, and I'll chop down trees. Believe me, I'm better with an ax than a plow."

Ian wagged his head from side to side. "Your plot is cleared; I need to clear stones. I—"

"Under the best of circumstances with a normal plow, I'd make a fool of myself. In the time it would take me to plow the garden with this contraption, you could have done yours, ours, and more too boot. We're simply trading skills."

"Tell you what: I'll clear stones while you catch more fish. I'm not looking to put in a huge garden—just enough to get by. Then we can start in on that deal."

Tucker chewed the inside of his cheek and looked at their claims. "How much seed did you bring?" A minute later, he cupped his hands and called, "Sis?"

Miss Smith came around the side of their cabin, her arms full of deadwood. "Yes?"

"C'mon over here." He cupped his chin in his hand and tapped his forefinger against his cheek as if he was pondering something perplexing.

Ian threw back his head and laughed. When Tucker looked at him as if he'd lost his senses, he smirked. "You just made a big mistake."

❧

Meredith dropped the wood and walked toward the men. Tucker was giving her the sign. Her brother was going to make some kind of a deal, and he wanted her to hear the bargaining and give her opinion. She respected that about her brother: he included her in decisions and tried hard to be scrupulously fair to whomever he dealt with.

"Sis, I think we need to come to an agreement with Ian. He brought enough seed to sow a good-sized garden, and he has his mule and this plow."

"A plow your brother helped construct."

Meredith looked at the strange creation. "That's, uh. . .quite a plow, Mr. Rafferty."

An impish twinkle lit his blue eyes. "You might say that."

"I proposed that if Ian would plow your garden in addition to his own, I'd spend the morning felling trees for his cabin."

"No, no." Mr. Rafferty started tapping his foot. "That's not right. I'll spend half the day clearing stones from the plot on my side. Yours is already clear."

"But you have the seeds. Sis, he's got seeds for everything from beets to radishes."

"Wonderful!" She brightened at that news. They'd had so little variation in their diet that even the smallest change thrilled her. "I have beans and cabbage."

"What kind of beans might they be?"

She smiled. "Green pod beans and yellow wax beans."

Tucker started pacing. "That's nice, Sis. It's a nice start. But it's not much. He's got everything. Carrots. Turnips. Table beets and lettuce and potatoes—and that's just part of it."

Watching her brother left her feeling slightly dizzy, so Meredith focused back on Mr. Rafferty. "Carrots? Oh, they sound delicious! And beets—it'll be so nice just to have color on our plates instead of white and brown food. I do hope it doesn't sound as if I'm complaining. Well, maybe I am, a little. But God's provided for us. We've had enough to eat."

"We'll plant plenty and store up sufficient for a long winter."

Tucker turned back around and headed toward them. "But your seeds and labor. Whatever is extra—"

"We'll sell or trade with our neighbors."

"That's a wonderful plan, Mr. Rafferty." Meredith started thinking of the things she'd put on the list of necessities. Maybe she could reduce some of the amounts if their garden grew bountifully.

"Your garden. Your plow." Tucker stepped closer to their new neighbor. "Your seeds. You—"

"I," Mr. Rafferty interrupted, "propose that we'll all labor and share equally in the yield."

"But there are two of us," Meredith pointed out. "We'll eat more."

"And unless I miss my guess, Miss Smith, you'll be far more efficient in making sure things are preserved."

Tucker didn't stop pacing. He walked toward the riverbank and back, each time expounding on a concept or challenging Mr. Rafferty's assertions and offers.

Mr. Rafferty continued to interrupt him. Of course, he couldn't stand still. That would have made it far too simple. He'd stoop and heft a rock, then pitch or carry it off a ways. With one man moving up and down while the other paced from side to side, Meredith found herself leaning on the crazy makeshift plow so she wouldn't be so dizzy.

"Well?" Tucker finally stopped.

"Do you agree, Miss Smith?" Both men looked at her.

"Let me get this straight." She shook her head to clear away the confusion. "You'll both build a smokehouse, which is to be spaced evenly between our homes. Since the fish are plentiful right now, you'll use the logs from the lean-to so the smokehouse will be ready tomorrow when Tucker returns from fishing all day. While my brother fishes, Mr. Rafferty will plow a garden—a large garden which is now marked by the four boulders he's laid out."

"Perhaps a wee bit larger," Mr. Rafferty mused.

Before Tucker could charge into further negotiations, Meredith blurted out, "Mr. Rafferty and I will sow the seeds, and we'll mind the garden. Because it's his plow and the lion's portion of the seeds is his, and he's doing half the labor, and there are two Smiths and only one Rafferty, I'll be in charge of preserving as much as possible for the cold months. Whatever excess produce might grow will be bartered or sold, with the proceeds being split evenly."

Just summing it all up exhausted her. Meredith sucked in a deep breath.

"I'm thinking it all sounds good so far." Mr. Rafferty nodded.

"I don't." Tucker started pacing again. "It's lopsided. We're taking advantage of you."

Mr. Rafferty cast an exasperated look at Meredith. "Explain the rest to your hardheaded brother. If anything, the deal's heavily weighted to my advantage. In fact, I think—"

"I think you both need to let me finish stating the agreement." Tucker escalated the speed of his pacing, and if Mr. Rafferty went back to rock clearing, she wouldn't be responsible for her actions. "Tucker, do stop wearing a path in the ground. I'm dizzy from watching you."

"Are you feeling poorly, Miss Smith?" Mr. Rafferty solicitously cupped her elbow as if she were a feeble grandmother.

"I knew it. Uncle Darian's is where you belong. It's too harsh up here for you." Tucker grabbed her other arm.

"Nonsense." Fearing she'd soon be caught in a tug o' war, she pulled away from both men. "I'm stronger than that mule."

"Maybe not as strong, but every bit as stubborn," Tucker mumbled.

"You're a braver man than I, Tucker. If I ever said something like that about my sister, Fiona, I'd never hear the last of it."

Meredith cocked a brow and glared at the men, who now stood side by side. She cleared her throat.

"Sore throat? I've some medicaments—"

"Nah," Tucker said, stopping Mr. Rafferty. "She likely needs a sip of water. I'll fetch it."

"So help me, if you so much as take one step away from here before we finish this deal and shake on it, I'll push you in that river, Tucker!" She shot Mr. Rafferty a look that dared him to say a single word.

The man had the audacity to grin at her like a simpleton.

"My brother will help you chop down trees and build your cabin—"

"The logs come off my property," Mr. Rafferty inserted.

Tucker nodded agreement, so Meredith continued. "In return for your assistance in putting a floor in our cabin—"

"Which will come from trees felled on our claim," Tucker said.

Meredith didn't bother to look at Mr. Rafferty. She rubbed her temple. "And Mr. Rafferty insists we receive half of whatever meat his hunting yields." She barely sucked in a breath and hurried on so they couldn't interrupt yet again. "During the next week or so while this construction is under way, I will prepare meals for the three of us using Mr. Rafferty's supplies. Thereafter, Tucker may ride Bess to town and use her to pack in our supplies. Furthermore, we are welcome to borrow your Bible unless you're reading it, which is at sunrise each day, but since sunrise is a ridiculous notion in Alaska, we will assume it to be at the outset of the morning. There. That had better be the end of this deal."

The new neighbor shook his head.

"What else, Mr. Rafferty?"

"Since you'll be preparing my meals—"

She lost all composure. "Seward bought Alaska from the

Russians with less trouble than this agreement!"

His eyes twinkled, and he nodded somberly. "And they called the purchase Seward's Folly. Well, all I wanted to say was that I'd take it as a favor if you'd call me Ian instead of Mr. Rafferty."

"If she calls you Ian, then you'll call my sister Meredith."

Afraid they'd plunge back into the bargaining they'd embraced with such relish, Meredith shouted, "That's it! We all have a deal."

"It blesses my heart to see you're so happy with it." Ian beamed.

Tucker bobbed his head in satisfaction.

Meredith stalked back toward the cabin muttering, "Alaska isn't going to turn me into a raving lunatic. It's the men who will!"

five

"Wastin' your time, I tell you!" Mr. Abrams shouted across the river. Water sloshed over the edge of the pan he swirled. "Two grown men playing house—that's what you are."

"He's a crazy old coot." The log slid into the notch with a solid thud. Tucker tacked on, "Nosy, too."

"A smokehouse, and now a cabin?" Abrams tutted loudly. "Next thing, it'll be a privy and a summer kitchen." The old man cackled as if he'd told a hilarious joke. "Yep. A summer kitchen. Because summers here are so long and hot!"

Ian shot Tucker a quick look. "A privy. I didn't think—"

"Chamber pot works fine."

Ian nodded curtly.

Abrams's cackling laugh drifted on the wind. "You'll still be roofin' that place when I move back to Seattle and live off my gold."

"Pay him no heed. He talks just to keep himself company."

Ian chuckled softly. "Had the Lord not blessed me with fine new neighbors, I might well have developed that same habit myself in a few years. As I've both a brother and a sister, I'm accustomed to being teased. As long as he's not holding that rifle of his, Abrams is harmless." He and Tucker lifted the next log and dropped it into place.

"His motto is 'Shoot all trespassers.'"

"I found that out firsthand. Tell me, how good of a shot is he?"

"He's as good a marksman as I am a plowboy."

"Speaking of which—"

"We're making good time on this." Tucker kicked a small chunk of wood out of the way and pretended Ian hadn't interrupted.

"Thanks to your help. But our deal was—"

"Ian, the ground was frozen solid. It would have taken dynamite, not a plow, to turn over the soil. The ground is still hard as rock. Give it another day or so."

Meredith ventured over. "Lunch is ready."

"It smells wonderful. Your brother and I've worked up an appetite."

As they finished eating, Meredith gave Tucker a tentative look. "Did you ask him?"

Tucker's face puckered as he thought for a moment.

"The laundry," Meredith reminded him softly. A fetching blush tinted her cheeks.

"Oh. Forgot about it." He turned to Ian. "Sis is doing laundry this afternoon. You're welcome to toss whatever you have in the wash pot."

Ian opened his mouth to accept, but Meredith's blush changed his mind. "Thank you for the kind offer, but I'll do my own."

"The wash pot will already be boiling," Tucker pointed out.

"Aye, it will." Ian smiled at Meredith. "And I'll thank you not to dump out the suds. Once you're done, I'll see to my own wash."

"Hey! Wily!" Abrams shouted.

"Where is he?" Meredith tilted her head.

"There. Rounding the river bend," Tucker responded.

Meredith's brow puckered. "Of course Wily is coming on the river. But where is Mr. Abrams?"

"Did you come to your senses?" Abrams hollered to Wily, who paddled his odd-looking boat closer. "I ain't choosy— beer, whiskey, vodka—"

Ian didn't bother to hide the astonishment in his voice. "Abrams is up in that red alder. The lowest branch."

Laughter bubbled out of Meredith.

Wily squinted toward Abrams's claim. "You're going to break your neck, you old fool."

"It'll be your fault for not bringin' me likker. I have to hang upside down to straighten out my spine bone."

"Men who drink spirits don't have a backbone," Wily shot back. He nodded his thanks as Ian reached out, took a rope, and tied the boat to shore. A young man jumped from the other end of the boat and tied it as well.

True to his threat, Mr. Abrams dangled by his knees from the branch.

Tucker's voice went wry. "Ian, don't reach for your bow and arrows. That's not a giant possum. That's just a crazy old coot."

"I ain't crazy. My back's painin' me, and since I don't have any medicinal spirits, I gotta resort to this."

"I'll make you a willow-bark tea."

"Won't help, Meredith." Abrams continued to hang there. "Standin' knee-deep in that icy water's gonna cripple me. I need a good belt of Oh-Be-Joyful every hour or so to keep my innards warm enough."

"This is my nephew, Joe." Wily gestured toward the young man. "He's normally on a trawler, but this load was too heavy for me to move alone."

"Thankful for your help." Ian shook Joe's hand, then grabbed the first bundle from Wily.

Tucker and Meredith stood on the bank and stared at him.

"Meredith, how's about you taking the list I have here and checking everything off so Mr. Rafferty knows I brought everything?"

"Why, yes. Of course I will."

"Sis doesn't need to check a list." Tucker stepped forward.

"You brought half a mercantile."

"The wrong half!" Abrams shouted. "It wouldn't have hurt to bring along a few bottles."

"One more thing, and the boat would have sunk." Tucker tromped toward Ian's claim.

Meredith accepted the list. "The flour and sugar are obvious, but how do you know what's in the crates?"

"I have them numbered."

Wily scratched his nose. "Didn't imagine you'd already have a cabin goin' up. We can just pass everything in so you don't have to move it again."

With four men unloading the supplies, things went smoothly. Joe elbowed Tucker. "Those stampeders walking the Chilkoot Trail are idiots. They have to carry caches, backtrack, and carry in more. Canada won't let 'em in without a ton of supplies."

"He's not exaggerating. Canadians demand a full ton. Nothing less, or the prospectors will starve." Wily thumped down a sack of cornmeal. "Might take you longer to coax as much gold from the ground here, but you'll still be alive."

Ian hefted another sack. "Tucker, since Meredith is cooking for us, it's stupid to keep all of this at my place. Let's take a bag each of flour, cornmeal, sugar, and beans over to your cabin."

Meredith ran her hand over a sack of flour. "Tucker, when you go to Goose Chase, try to buy flour in this sack if you can. It's pretty."

"Rafferty came up here with his supplies." Joe trudged past with a washtub full of sundry items. "Socks doesn't have anything like that."

A look of disappointment flickered across her features, but if Ian hadn't been facing her, he knew he wouldn't have seen it. She shoved a pin back into her bun to keep it anchored. "I suppose I ought to be thankful Socks has flour at all!"

Ian decided he'd give Meredith the sacks—but he'd wait until he could "bargain" with her so she wouldn't feel as if he was treating her like a charity case. He gave her a quizzical look. "Socks?"

"The owner of the mercantile in town." She smiled at him—a warmhearted smile that proved she'd already set aside her disappointment. "Rumor has it that he was so cold his first winter up here, he unraveled a pair of socks and knit them into a hat."

"He knit something, himself?" Ian couldn't imagine a man fiddling with yarn and knitting needles.

"It's a fact, not a rumor." Wily shook his head. "Never saw a man more proud of himself. He wouldn't take off that hat. Come summer, Socks finally peeled off the ugly thing. He'd gone bald as an egg. We tease him and say he ought to have washed the socks before he made them into a hat."

"He couldn't afford his own soap to wash 'em. Prices on everything are sky high." Joe shook his head. "The trawler I work—the captain said he'll keep us in coffee, but we have to drink it black now because sugar is twenty-five cents a pound."

Meredith gasped.

Joe nodded. "Yep. And it's fifty cents for one can of condensed milk."

The strained grooves bracketing Tucker's mouth told Ian the Smiths hadn't mined enough gold to buy supplies at those outrageous rates. He'd read about the inflated prices and hedged against that eventuality by paying shipping for his provender.

"Good thing you're such a fisherman." Ian slapped Tucker on the back. "I haven't hunted yet because everything is scrawny in the springtime. Come autumn, I'll see about bagging a mountain sheep or two, some pheasant, and plump hares."

"With all of that and our garden, we'll be well set." Meredith nodded.

"Garden?" Perplexed lines carved Wily's face.

"Aye." Ian gestured toward the area behind the smokehouse. "I'll be plowing that field in the next few days. Meredith and I are planning to sow a bounty of vegetables."

"My ma lives in Skaguay. She roped me into helping her plant every year." Joe shrugged. "Now all I do is take fish heads and guts home to her. She claims it makes everything grow better."

"Aye, and she's right." Ian nodded. "Fish enrich the soil."

Meredith tugged on Tucker's sleeve. "All the more reason to give thanks that you're such a good fisherman."

"Didn't realize the fishing around here is so good." Wily gazed at the river.

"I don't have to be back until Friday, Uncle, but I pull in nets of fish every day. Don't expect me to join you." Joe cast a glance at the partially built cabin. "Don't mean to sound boastful, but the fact is, I'm good with an ax. I've won contests. Trees don't stand a chance around me."

A sick feeling hit the bottom of Ian's stomach. He hated admitting how little money he had left. "I, ah. . .don't know what the going rate—"

Joe reared back. "I'm offering my help. I don't want to be paid. This is Alaska. We help our neighbors!"

"I meant no offense, and I'll gladly accept your help."

Wily cocked his head to the side. "It's past noontime. Dawn's the best time to fish. Those are some nice, straight logs over yonder. I could split them—maybe even get a few planks for you."

Thrilled by that offer, Ian seized it. "We promised Meredith a plank floor for her cabin."

Meredith blinked, then shook her head emphatically. "Getting a roof over your head is far more important."

"Those logs are from your property." Tucker scowled at him.

Ian shrugged. "So you'll trade me for some from yours."

Meredith started to back away. "Oh no! Wily, Joe—run quick! Once Tucker and Ian start bargaining, they don't stop."

"I tell you what." Ian grinned. "We'll just leave that as the only swap as long as you agree to cook for Wily and Joe, too."

"Of course I'll cook for them. What kind of hostess do you think I am?"

Ian didn't hesitate for a single second. "The grandest in all of Alaska."

"That's not saying much." She arched a brow. "There are probably all of ten women in the whole region."

"Other women heard of your gracious talent and stayed away because they couldn't bear the thought of falling short of your example."

"That proves it." She turned to Tucker. "You said he's a Scot, but he's not. Only an Irishman would be so full of blarney."

"You thought I'm a Scot?" Ian growled at Tucker. "That's nearly as bad as the insult your sister just gave me."

"Scots are good men." Tucker sounded downright bored. "What insult?"

"Scots might well be good, but Irishmen are grand. 'Tis no more a boast than Joe's telling us he's capable with an ax." Ian turned his attention back to Meredith. "But I'll not stand here and have you consider my praise as bluster or blarney. With your merry heart and willing hands, you're a rare woman. 'Tisn't the fare or china on the table that makes a body feel welcome. Like the proverb in the Bible, I'd far rather have a humble meal of herbs with pleasant company than a feast where there's strife."

"I agree." Wily clapped his hands and rubbed them together. "But we'll see about adding a plank floor to that cabin. Where are the tools?"

Ian grabbed a couple of axes and headed toward the woods with Joe. Joe tested the weight of one ax and mused, "Meredith Smith is a spirited woman."

"Indeed, she is."

"I've only seen her once before. She's certainly worth a second look."

Ian locked eyes with Joe. "She's adventurous and friendly, but Meredith Smith is every inch a lady."

A lazy smile tilted one corner of Joe's mouth. "I wondered if you were taken with her. Can't blame you." His ax bit into a tree trunk.

Ian paced to the other side of the tree and started swinging the other ax. Until now, he'd focused on the tasks at hand. Suddenly, the truth struck him. He'd come on the journey of his life and found a woman whose sense of adventure matched his own. From times of prayer and Bible reading, he knew she loved the Lord. With each blow of his ax, he listed her qualities—her virtuous ways, her kind heart, her warm smile, the sunny outlook she maintained—

"Hey!"

Ian gave Joe a startled look.

"Step aside. This one's ready to go."

Ian joined Joe on the other side of the trunk. "Timber!" he bellowed. Then they nudged the trunk above where they'd chopped. Branches rustled, air whistled through the limbs, and the last bit of the trunk cracked as the tree plunged down.

"That one fell hard and fast."

Ian nodded as he continued to think of Meredith. *So did I.*

six

Meredith waved. "God go with you!" Wily and Joe's umiak floated around the river's bend and out of sight.

Behind her, Ian nickered to Bess. He'd already plowed two rows since breakfast—a true feat considering the still-frosty ground and the odd "plow" he'd concocted.

Meredith turned and watched as the fabric of his shirt went taut over muscles in his arms and shoulders. He fought the stubborn soil, and Bess strained, but inch by inch, foot by foot, they made progress.

Carrying a washtub filled with sand, Tucker staggered past Meredith.

"Let me help!"

"Open the door. It blew shut."

Meredith dashed ahead and yanked open the door to their cabin. Each evening, the men had dragged stones into the cabin and cobbled a section of the floor. As dawn broke to-day, they'd dragged out what little furniture she and Tucker owned and carried in logs split in half. Those puncheons now formed a real floor, but instead of staying steady like planks would have, the puncheons rocked and tilted.

Grunting, Tucker dumped the sand onto the floor. He cast a look at the door. "Sis, Rafferty's a fine man."

She blushed. "That's my assessment, too."

"But I don't care how nice he is. You made a promise to me, and I expect you to keep it."

"I haven't said a word to him."

Tucker hefted the empty bucket. "Don't. Some things stay

in the family. It's no one else's business."

She hitched her shoulder. "It doesn't matter to me, Tucker. It's important to you, so I'll stay quiet."

"Good." He stared at her, looking as though he expected her to say more.

"I'll work the sand into the floor." Meredith dragged her instep across a ribbon of sand and watched it filter through the cracks. "I'm starting to notice a difference. The sand's keeping the logs from rolling and tilting so much."

Tucker heaved a sigh. He knew her well enough to see that she'd changed the subject. But she'd told him she'd stay quiet, so he went on to the new topic. "Even when I get the puncheons stabilized, the floor'll be rough, Sis. You're liable to get splinters in your feet."

"Nonsense. You men used files and rasps to smooth the surface, and the sand will take care of most of the tiny stickers. I'll braid a nice, warm rug to go between our beds, and we'll be snug as can be."

"We don't have cloth for that."

She flashed her twin a smile. "Anything worth having is worth waiting for."

Tucker snorted and tromped back outside to fetch more sand.

After building a fire and setting the huge wash kettle over it, Meredith hung the quilts out to air. The laundry she'd planned to do days ago desperately needed to be done. In the past, she'd hung her unmentionables in the cabin by the fire to dry. Fearing Ian would take a notion to help her brother with the floor, Meredith decided she'd better hang her small clothes on a line between the quilts. With Tucker's shirts on one side and britches on the other, no one would be able to spy her garments.

As Meredith rinsed the whites, Tucker began to whistle

softly. *"Rock of Ages, cleft for me. . ."* The hymn's lyrics ran through her mind.

"Let me hide myself in thee," Ian sang. Or at least, that's what Meredith thought he was trying to do. Not even two of those words were sung in the same key.

"Sis, forget the laundry." Tucker hauled more sand. "Hurry up and make lunch so he'll stop singing."

Ian had his back to them and continued to plow as he caterwauled, "Let the water and the blood, from Thy wounded side which flowed. . ."

Tucker winced. "Sounds like blood's flowing, all right. Just not the sacred variety."

"Be of sin the double cure. . ."

"I never would have guessed it, but Abrams is right," Tucker muttered. "Some afflictions deserve a stiff belt of whiskey."

Meredith giggled. "I don't think whiskey can cure that."

"It wouldn't be for him—it would be for everyone who has to listen."

Straightening up, Meredith wrung out a petticoat. "Bess doesn't seem to mind."

"Dumb mule doesn't know any better. I mean it, Sis. Take pity on me and make lunch. It'll stop him from—"

"Singing?" she filled in.

"I refuse to lie and call that singing."

"Are you sick or just dying?" Abrams shouted across the river.

Ian halted mid-row. "Someone's sick?"

"You gotta be. Ain't never heard sounds like that come outta someone unless they was sufferin' real bad."

"He's going to say something about spirits," Meredith whispered to her brother.

"Couple of stiff swigs of whiskey would fix your throat. I'm telling you, Wily needs to deliver spirits to us. They're medicinal."

"Nothing's wrong with my throat." Ian stretched his back.

"That's a matter of opinion." Tucker set down the bucket of sand.

"Had a gelding break a leg once." Abrams continued to swish water and silt in his mining pan. "Sounded just like you. I put him outta his misery."

"I guess I should be thankful you're holding a pan instead of your rifle." Ian's voice held an entertained lilt.

Meredith couldn't help wondering, *How can he have such a deep, true speaking voice yet sing so dreadfully?*

Tucker rested his hands on his hips. "Do you whistle or hum any better than you sing?"

"Nope." Ian grinned like the Cheshire cat from *Alice's Adventures in Wonderland.* "I'm so tone deaf, I got out of having to suffer through music lessons. I take heart in the verse that says, 'Make a joyful noise unto the Lord.'"

"It's noise, all right," Tucker said.

"Sounds like someone's slaughtering you." Abrams dumped out the last of his pan. He'd gotten nothing for his efforts. "Take pity on the rest of us. Call it Christian charity."

Ian's grin widened. "In Luke 19, Christ said if men were silenced, even the rocks would cry out His praise. I take it you'd rather hear the rocks?"

"No one means to insult you," Meredith said.

"Speak for yourself." Abrams scooped up another pan full of silt. "Maybe if the rocks cried, they'd be tears of gold."

"For that, I'd keep my silence." Ian nickered to Bess and flicked the reins. As his plow split the stubborn earth, he disappeared behind the smokehouse.

"Do you still want lunch right away?"

Tucker looked at the little droplets of mud her dripping petticoat created on the ground between them. "Nah. Go on ahead and finish whatever you need to."

After lunch, Meredith shoved her hands in her apron pockets. "Ian, the wash pot is empty now."

"Good. I've gotten to the point that I wouldn't have to put pegs on the walls to hang my clothes. They're all about to stand up on their own. Since we're using your wood and soap this time, next time we'll use mine."

"Meredith!" Abrams bellowed from his side of the river. "I gotta little laundry. Some mending, too. What's your asking price?"

Unladylike as shouting was, she walked toward the riverbank and modulated her voice. "How much mending?"

"Some buttons. A few rips, and my socks need darning."

"How many rips and buttons, and do you still have the buttons?"

Mr. Abrams looked like a sulky toddler who'd been caught tugging on the dog's tail. "You can't expect a man to remember where stupid little buttons roll off to."

"I don't have many spare buttons."

"I'll pay you a pinch of gold dust for it all."

Meredith laughed. "You'd pay that much for one splash of whiskey in town."

"It's going to take all my gold to buy vittles for next year."

"Provender is expensive." She nodded. "Tucker was saying the very same thing. It's going to take all we have to supply us for the next year, too."

"You're putting in a garden. That'll cut your costs. Two pinches, and that's as much as I'll offer."

"You have months' worth of grime in those clothes, so it's going to take me half of forever to wash and mend them. Four."

"Four!" Abrams roared.

"Or. . ." She paused.

"Or?"

"You come help put the roof on Ian's cabin and allow us free transit across your claim whenever we go to town."

"Do I look like a carpenter to you?" He spread out his arms, and water sloshed from his gold pan onto his sleeve and back into the river.

"You're a man of many talents, I'm sure." She smiled. "And though I don't wish to be rude, you are a man in sore need of a woman's assistance. Your clothes are in tatters."

Ian wandered over and stood beside her. "You don't have do pay the man to help me, Meredith. 'Tisn't right."

"I'd do his laundry anyway, Ian."

He shot her a sideways glance. "Self-preservation?"

"Precisely."

Ian grinned. "Abrams—let's make this deal better for everyone involved."

Abrams brightened. "You do have some whiskey, after all!"

"No, no." Ian folded his arms across his chest. "What I have in mind is a far better proposition."

"Ain't nothin' better than a coupla long swigs of Who-Hit-John."

Ian ignored Abrams's grumble. "You'll provide the logs to make a pontoon bridge across the river, and—".

"A bridge? I'm a miner, not a carpenter. I need to spend my time prospecting."

"Just listen. The river's about twenty feet from here to there. One of those spruces on your claim will more than do the trick. Just a medium one."

"How do you reckon that?"

"I'll help you cut the lower portion into four pontoons, and we'll split the rest of the trunk in half lengthwise to lie over them."

"Why bother splitting it?"

"For Meredith." He cupped his hand on her shoulder. Big as

his hand was, he didn't rest the weight there. Warmth radiated from him, though.

It wasn't just physical warmth. A sense of his kindness washed over her. She'd never once said a word to Tucker about how she was stranded on this side of the river. Ian understood the issue and created a solution.

Speaking in a man-to-man tone, he continued to address Abrams. "We need to make sure Meredith will have secure footing when she crosses. Splitting the log and placing the puncheons side by side ought to make the bridge wide enough. In fact, due to her full skirts, a rail might be smart."

"No. No rail. A rope is good enough." Abrams's face grew dark. "But what do I get out of this?"

"You"—Ian stretched out the word as though he were preparing to crown a king—"may use Bess to go into Goose Chase and back on the day of your choosing next week. With your back paining you as much as it does, I know it would help for a sturdy mule like Bess to haul your supplies."

"That's very generous of you." Meredith smiled at Ian. "Bess is a fine mule."

"Aye, she is. And by next week, I'll have finished plowing and dragging timber."

"Compared to the time it would take you to do your laundry, mend your clothes, and make several trips to Goose Chase to bring back supplies," Tucker said as he scooped up more sand, "one day of roofing and a few hours to make a bridge is nothing."

As Ian withdrew his hand, Meredith fought the urge to lean toward him to prolong the contact. Instead, she concentrated on the old man across the river. "My brother is right. That trade is heavily in your favor, Mr. Abrams."

"I dunno." Abrams combed his fingers through his grungy beard.

"Well, don't worry about it." Ian turned to Meredith. Mirth crinkled the corners of his oh-so-blue eyes. "I'm sure whoever is across the river from my claim will be more than happy—"

"Hang on a minute. A man deserves a minute to think through a deal." Abrams bobbed his head. "Yup. I'll do it. But if Wily gets het up about you blocking the river so he can't take that sorry excuse for a boat any farther, you gotta deal with him."

"Wily won't mind," Tucker said. "He never goes any farther upriver than Clemment's."

Mr. Abrams let out a cackle. "He'll take it as a favor. Nobody wants to deal with that crazy old coot!"

"It's not a problem. With a pontoon bridge, we can let one end float downstream and pull it back in place after Wily's boat goes through," Ian reasoned.

"The real problem will be Abrams." The corners of Tucker's mouth tightened. "The minute that bridge is built, he'll come tromping over every time he smells coffee or food."

"What if we make a deal where we won't cross onto his claim, and he won't come over here, unless we've gotten permission?" Meredith shrugged. "It's good manners."

Tucker snorted. "Abrams wouldn't know good manners if they bit him."

"How would the two of you feel about telling him he's invited to Sunday supper each week—provided he worship with us first?" Ian hooked his thumbs in the pockets of his jeans. "The rest of the week, we'll have the bridge float along our side of the river. I'll link it from the midpoint of my claim so you won't feel it's impinging on your panning, and Abrams won't worry about whether it diverts any gold that would flow his way."

"What are you all yammerin' about over there?" Abrams scowled.

"My brother and Ian are making sure everything will work

out fairly." Meredith gestured toward the river. "They're concerned that the bridge might block the flow to your bank and affect how much gold you wind up with."

"Then there ain't gonna be no bridge!"

"We worked it all out," Ian declared. "The bridge will normally float parallel to our shore. Whenever we need to cross, we'll pulley it into place."

"Humph."

"But we'll worship every Sunday, and you're invited to join us." Seeing the horror on the old man's face, Meredith hurriedly tacked on, "And of course you'd be welcome to stay for Sunday supper."

"I ain't makin' no promises."

"Take your time. You can decide from week to week." Tucker wrapped his arm around her shoulders. "But you know what a fine cook Sis is."

"Aye, that she is!" Ian turned to her. "Why don't you go ahead and see to our neighbor's laundry? It's silly for me to wash my clothes when I still have plowing to finish."

"I am looking forward to having a garden."

Ian smiled at her. "Good. I'm thinking 'tis a shame, though, that I didn't bring any flower seeds. Ma always likes to plant a patch."

"Soon we'll have flowers all about us. Alaska is harsh, but wildflowers abound."

"I should have known." Ian studied her for a long moment. "The fairest of all are brought about by God's hand."

Meredith felt her face grow warm. Men in the region dropped by and tried to flatter her in hopes of getting a meal or a cheaper rate on mending. In the thirteen months since she'd been in Alaska, never once had a man complimented her without having an ulterior motive. Ian walked away before she could form a response.

seven

I shouldn't have said anything. Not so soon. I've barely met the lass. Ian tied twine to an arrow and shot it over onto Abrams's property. *I embarrassed her. She's too kind to say so, but her blush made it clear as day.*

"I'll send a rope over now." Tucker attached rope to the twine. "It's best if Abrams ties the rope on his side first. I aim to yank hard when I secure it on this side. That way, if he didn't do a decent job, nothing is lost when it gives way." Tucker paused a second. "I can't help thinking, though, it might be a blessing if his laundry took a dunking before Sis has to wash it."

Ian looked up at the clouds and started whistling. He turned and walked off.

"Ian!" Tucker shouted at him. "You can't whistle any better than you sing!"

"Want me to start humming instead?"

"Spare me the agony."

Ian considered humming just for fun, but he had to harness Bess to the plow. Bess didn't like his music any better than Tucker did, so Ian decided garnering her cooperation was more important than needling Tucker.

Plowing the virgin soil took great effort. Even the best plow would be tested by the plot, and Ian ruefully fought to keep control over the rudimentary one he'd designed. The soil looked rich, though. Each foot would mean another cabbage. Each yard would support a trellis of climbing beans. As the crops grew, he'd be able to spend time with Meredith. Perhaps then, if he were patient, he'd reap more than just vegetables. If God willed it, Ian hoped to cultivate Meredith's affection, too.

"Just how much more do you plan to do?" Tucker leaned against the smokehouse and scanned the garden.

"May as well do a few extra rows. I was thinking that when you go to town, you could see if they have any of the seeds from Sitka."

"What does Sitka have to do with seeds?"

"The Russians settled here first. I read that the czar ordered each settlement had to have a garden. Since America bought the land, the government decided the Russians had a good notion. Sitka sends out seeds for free. I'm thinking Meredith might like some parsley and mustard. Rhubarb, too."

"Rhubarb!" Tucker moaned. "I don't remember the last time I had rhubarb pie. Maybe you ought to plow twice as much."

Ian opened his mouth to reply, but the plow caught on a stone and veered to the side. "Looks like you're out of luck. The soil's shallow and rocky here."

"What about another row farther back?"

"Sure, and why not? We may as well coax as much as we can from the land. How's Meredith's new floor?"

"Done." Tucker looked at his cabin. "Nothing shifts when I walk across it. I'll lead Bess over to the back of the plot. You bring the plow."

A moment later, Ian set down the plow. "We've got a good six feet here. I can get at least three more rows in. Maybe four."

"With the size root cellars we both have, you'd better make it four. I figure we'll finish off your cabin tomorrow; then I'll go to Goose Chase. If there's anything you need, write it down. I'll try to get it for you."

"I'll think on it. Ho, there, Bess. All right, girl. Let's go." He clicked his tongue, and his mule started pulling the plow.

That row was difficult. The next fought him even more. Halfway across, Bess stopped dead in her tracks.

"Aww, c'mon, Bess." Ian jostled the reins.

Her tail started to spin in a circle—a sure sign she'd made up her mind and wasn't in any mood to listen to his plans. "Bessie, Bessie, Bessie," he crooned.

She turned to the side and gave him a baleful glare. Mules in general, and Bess in particular, would hit a point where they got tired and simply refused to work another minute. Her scraggly tail spun again.

"All right. You've done all you can today." Ian released the plow and walked up to give her an appreciative pat on the withers. "You're a good girl. You've worked hard."

Freed from her obligations, Bess wandered away. Ian hung the harness on the hefty pegs he'd driven into the outside of the smokehouse. He paced back to the plow. Leaving it in place was okay, but he needed to scrape off the worst of the muck so it wouldn't dry and turn into a heavy, jagged crust.

"Done?" Meredith asked.

"Not yet. Bess decided she'd worked enough for the day, so I'll finish the last two rows first thing tomorrow." He scraped off one last glop. "How's the laundry going?"

"My laundry line is full. I wanted to know if you'd mind me pinning clothes to the rope over the river."

"I don't think that's the best idea."

Meredith wrinkled her nose. "I understand. I was afraid something might fall in."

"Not something. Someone." Straightening up, Ian slid his knife back into the belt sheath. "Clothes can be replaced. Fast and cold as that water is, we can't risk you. I'll string up something."

"We don't have any more rope, Ian."

"Ah, but lass, I have wire. It ought to serve." He located

the crate containing the wire, and Meredith decided where she wanted him to string it. Cheery as a lark, she chattered and laughed as he wound the wire securely around a branch. When Ian reached to secure the second side, Tucker shouted his name.

"What?" Ian called back.

"Get over here." Tucker stood with his arms akimbo. His voice sounded harsh as a whip. "We've got to have a talk."

Until now, Tucker had been a shade taciturn. Wry, too. But he'd never been overbearing. *He's protective of his sister. He doesn't want me around her.* Ian decided to finish his task. "I'll be over in a minute."

"Now," Tucker ground out.

eight

"Something's wrong." Meredith scurried toward her brother. Ian hastened alongside her.

Tucker stepped back into the shade behind the smokehouse. He yanked her arm and shoved her past himself.

"That's no way to treat a lady!" Ian glowered at Tucker.

Ignoring Ian's protest, Tucker rasped harshly, "Look."

"Ian's done a wonderful job, Tucker." Meredith gave her brother a puzzled glance. "It'll be a fine garden, indeed."

"No, it won't."

"Tucker, you can't say that. We have solid plans."

Ian hunkered down, then shot to his feet. "We'll change our plans."

Meredith gawked at him. "What has gotten into the two of you?"

Ian held out his hand. A small white stone with a tiny thread of color was nestled in his palm. "Gold fever."

Staring at his hand, Meredith tried not to let her hope run amok. That one small glint of yellow wasn't enough to sneeze at.

"Look." Tucker stooped down and brushed away more dirt. "White quartz. Gold is most often found in white quartz."

"The vein is slim as a cobweb, but it's there." Excitement pulsed in Ian's voice. "Glory be to God!"

Tucker rose and wiped his fingers off on his pants. He stuck out his hand. "Congratulations, Rafferty. You've struck gold."

Meredith shot a startled look toward the woods. Tucker was right. The quartz was a solid four feet from the property line—and on Ian's claim.

Ian extended his right hand, clasped Tucker's, and shook. "Aye, we've struck gold."

Lord, look at Tucker. He's trying so hard to be honorable. You know how much he needed that gold. But if someone else is to have it, there's no finer man than Ian Rafferty. Meredith swallowed the bitter taste of disappointment. "You're right. The plans will change now. Ian won't need a garden."

"Nonsense!" Ian turned loose of Tucker's hand and faced her. "We'll need good, hearty food to prospect. It's just that instead of coaxing mustard yellow from this spot, we'll mine gold!"

Meredith managed a tipsy smile. "That was clever. We're very happy for you, Ian."

His brows knit. "For me?" His eyes widened. "Oh no. No, no, no. This belongs to all of us."

"It's on your claim." Tucker sounded as if he'd backed into cactus.

"And you discovered it." Ian folded his arms across his chest. "I'm going to be stubborn, so you'd best just agree. This is a fifty/fifty partnership."

"Don't be a fool." Tucker turned and started to walk off.

"Tucker Smith, we struck a bargain. I'm holding you to your word. You are a man of your word, aren't you?"

Meredith gasped.

Tucker wheeled around. "You're questioning my honor?"

A slow smile lifted the corners of Ian's mouth. "You agreed that anything coming from the garden would be split half and half. An honorable man's word is his bond. Either you stick with that bargain, or you renege. What's it going to be?"

"It's not that clear-cut."

Ian turned toward her. "It's plain as can be to me. You were there. Did your twin agree to an even split?"

Unsure of how to answer, Meredith tried to recall exactly

what they'd said. Part of her wanted to agree with Ian and remove some of the financial burden from Tucker's shoulders. On the other hand, she didn't want to take what wasn't rightfully theirs. "We were discussing the garden. We said we'd all labor and share equally in the yield, but—"

"There's no *but*. We agreed." Ian's smile would be smug if he weren't being so astonishingly generous. He looked from her to Tucker and back again. "I'm holding you to your word."

"All our neighbors combined aren't as demented as you are." Tucker stared at Ian. "We don't expect you to do this. The discussion was about produce, not gold."

"Yield." Ian stared her brother in the eyes. "I distinctly remember the word *yield*, and so does your sister. The matter is settled. We are going to have one problem, though."

Tucker looked wary. "What's that?"

"Abrams. The minute he comes across the bridge and sees this, he'll be a problem. I can just imagine him going to Goose Chase, getting soused at the saloon, and blabbing."

"So he won't know about it." Meredith reached up and tucked an escaping tendril of hair behind her ear. As soon as she finished the mundane task, she realized Ian was watching her intently. *What is he thinking? The other men in the area all want to marry me to ease their lives. Ian hasn't said a thing, and he's even doing his own laundry. He isn't like anyone else. I can't figure him out.*

"Why not?" He still didn't stop gazing at her.

"Why not?" Meredith echoed as she scrambled to recall what they'd been conversing.

"My guess is, Sis figures Abrams will think you're spending all sorts of time gardening."

"Exactly!" Relief flooded her.

"That excuse won't last long."

Tucker shrugged. "No, but it'll at least last through next

week. By then, he'll have gone to town and returned. Meredith and I have been panning at the river's edge. A few prospectors in the region are digging shafts. With you being new to the claim, no one will give a whole lot of thought to you going about things your own way."

"Good." Ian smiled. "You asked if there was anything I wanted from town. Another pickax would be smart. A sledgehammer, too."

"I have both." The tiniest bit of pride rang in Tucker's voice.

"Now how do you like that?" Ian's eyes twinkled. "The partnership couldn't be off to any better start than that!"

"One more thing. I'm holding you to your word, too." Tucker jabbed his forefinger at Ian. "You said if the rocks cried out, you wouldn't sing. Well, the rocks cried out. I personally think it's God's way of sparing Meredith and me from having to hear you slaughter tunes."

"Well, now, you do have a point." Ian scuffed his boot in the overturned soil. "I won't sing."

"Fine." Tucker walked off.

Ian winked at Meredith. "You're my witness, lass. I vowed I'd not sing. I said nothing about whistling or humming."

❧

Ian admired his handiwork. Meredith would be so pleased when she saw what he'd made! He'd encouraged her to go to town with Tucker yesterday. They'd be back late this afternoon.

Ian stepped backward. *Squish.* He gritted his teeth at the disgusting sound. Distracted as he was, he'd gone directly into a puddle of mud that now threatened to suck off his boot. *It'll be too hard for Meredith to walk back on paths like this in one day. It might be tomorrow ere they return. All the better. I'll get more done and surprise her.*

Two days ago, while Tucker, Abrams, and he had roofed his new cabin, Meredith had planted her cabbage and beans.

Ian fought with himself whether to plant the rest of the seeds and surprise her, or to wait and have an excuse to spend time in the garden with her. In the end, he compromised and planted potatoes and carrots in her absence. The rest they'd do together.

Spending the last two nights under his own roof had felt odd. Lonely. While he'd slept outside by the fire, the arrangement seemed temporary. A whole canopy of stars kept him company. But sleeping indoors—well, it didn't seem right for the house to be so impossibly still.

Back home, Da snored. Ma often mumbled in her sleep. Fiona's bed creaked in protest when she'd flop over to be closer to her lamp so she could read late at night. The only other time he'd felt this way was when Braden married and moved from the room they'd shared and carried Maggie over the threshold of the small cabin next to the farmhouse.

What would it be like to marry Meredith and start a family here? Though larger than the Smiths' cabin, Ian's still wouldn't be big enough to hold the big family he hoped to have. *When the time comes, I'll add on.*

His stomach rumbled. Ian headed back into his house to rustle up something to eat. He'd burned the cornmeal mush for breakfast. That experience made him decide he'd probably do no better cooking in a fireplace than he did over the fire pit he currently used. When Abrams went to town next week, Ian would have him post a letter. He'd already sent one with Meredith—a short one that reassured Ma that he was safe and had good Christian neighbors and a sound roof over his head. The next letter would give Ma a special task: Send a stove!

He'd never given much thought to how hard Ma worked at the stove to cook. Meredith made it look easy as could be to throw together delicious meals at the hearth in her cabin. After a prolonged search, Ian found the recipe book Ma had created just for him to bring along.

Twenty-five minutes later, he peered into the pot and wondered why the rice looked so soupy.

Abrams lumbered across the bridge and sniffed. "I reckoned you'd be gettin' vittles. What're you making?"

"A mess."

The old man sauntered closer. "A mess of what?"

"It's supposed to be rice."

"Looks like a bowl of maggots."

Ian slapped the lid back on the pot.

"Squirrel. That's what we need. Chuck in some squirrel meat, and it'll be a fine stew. Grab that bow and arrows of yours. I don't wanna wait all day. I'm hungry."

Ian's stomach growled. "You know how to make stew?"

"Yep. Any idjit can. Just dump in the right stuff, and there you have it." Abrams pulled the rice from the fire. "Gotta set that aside, else it'll burn."

Abrams proved to be astonishingly adept at cooking. By the time Ian skinned and chopped one squirrel, Abrams had done the other two. "Son, gotta tell you, that squirrel is lucky he died quick from your arrow. Nothing deserves to be hacked up like that. It woulda been called torture if he was still alive."

"It'll still taste good."

"No thanks to you. We need a pinch of salt and a dash of pepper. What other seasonings d'ya have?"

"What else do you want?"

"Sage and thyme. Onion, if you've got one."

Almost an hour later, Ian slapped another glob of mud over the twigs he'd jammed into the spaces between the logs of his cabin. Chinking the cabin was essential—but it didn't take his mind off the delectable aroma wafting from the pot. "Abrams, I'm washing my hands. After that, I'm going to dive headfirst into that stew."

"It'll be ready by then."

As they sat and ate, Ian motioned toward the pot with his spoon. "If I didn't know just how tired Meredith and Tucker will be when they get back, I'd eat every last drop and lick that pot."

"We could make a second pot for them."

Abrams looked dead earnest, but Ian decided to treat his remark like a joke. He chortled. "You've a fine sense of humor."

"Well, you got a lotta food, you know."

"Not really. I brought what the recommendations are for one man for a year."

"I watched when you unloaded all the stuff Wily delivered. You brought more'n two hundred pounds of sugar and least a hundred pounds of cornmeal 'stead of fifty."

"I did." Ian nodded. "But I brought less canned fish and meat. I'm also hoping to grow more vegetables. Tucker and Meredith have advised me to ration my food very carefully, and I figure they know what they're talking about."

"Humph." He scraped the bottom of his bowl. "You can't be sure they'll be back today."

Instead of arguing, Ian changed the topic. "Do you have any empty bottles on your claim?"

"A few. Why?" Abrams squinted. "Don't tell me you're gonna wrap yourself up in a temperance banner and preach all the evils of alcohol. I'm a grown man. I can do whatever I please."

"It's not for me to condemn you. I wouldn't mind having some empty bottles, though."

"Most of 'em don't got a lid anymore. And if you're plannin' to store food in 'em, it won't work. They're nothing but trash."

"I see." Ian stood. "Well, I suppose we can leave the pot off in the ashes and hope the stew tastes half as good at suppertime as it did for lunch."

"Better. The longer it rests, the move flavor you get." Abrams stood up. "I'll bring some bottles when I come for supper."

Ian smothered a smile. It didn't escape his notice that Abrams had invited himself to supper. Anticipating that had prompted him to bag three squirrels at the outset. "You do that."

"We gonna have coffee?"

"Might. Then again, might not. How many bottles do you have? I'm talking quart-sized, not dinky, piddling ones. Round ones."

"Dunno. I'll check." Abrams scuttled back across the bridge. Ian went back to chinking his cabin.

"Six," Abrams shouted. "I got six so far."

"Is that all?" Ian didn't doubt for a moment that Abrams had plenty more. For the rest of the afternoon, Abrams kept hollering as he scrounged up more bottles, and Ian would simply nod.

"Twenty-nine! Dunno why you want 'em, but that's gotta be all I've got."

"Twenty-nine?"

"You wantin' 'em round's gonna give me fits. I never paid any mind to how many things come in rectangular bottles."

"Bring over everything you've got."

"Shoulda said so in the first place." Glass clinked in the metal washtub as Abrams crossed the bridge. It took him three trips to tote over an eye-popping assortment of bottles that once held everything from beer to whiskey, cod liver oil to hair tonic. The empty containers turned a patch of dirt into a glittering heap. "That's a lot of bottles. You have to admit, it's a fine assortment."

Ian gave Abrams a good-natured shove on the shoulder. "At lunch, you said they were trash."

"I gave up valuable time I coulda spent panning for gold.

My time's worth plenty."

"I agree. We'll have coffee after supper tonight."

Abrams's eyes narrowed. "Strong coffee—not that stingy, dishwater-weak brew."

"Strong enough to float a horseshoe. Between now and then, I have work to do."

Abrams shook his head. "Work is prospectin'. I have yet to see you work a lick. If all you wanted was to be a farmer, you shoulda settled somewhere else."

"My family has a grand farm in Oregon. I wanted something more, something different."

"Sure don't look that way," Abrams muttered as he left.

Ian stared down at the bottles. As he'd expected, most of them had once held spirits. Those didn't capture Ian's attention. He stared at the other ones. Braden insisted upon Maggie's taking a daily dose of Dr. Barker's Blood Builder because she'd always been on the delicate side. Fiona used Princess Tonic Hair Restorer. It seemed ludicrous that old Abrams used both of those products, too—but the proof lay there. On occasion, Da used Peptonic Stomach Bitters. Ma insisted that everyone take a teaspoon of Norwegian cod liver oil each morning. Odd, how ordinary glass bottles would bring back so many memories.

Ian surveyed his claim. Much as he hated to admit it, Abrams had a point. Like a good farmer, Ian had come, built a sturdy home, seen to a smokehouse, and plowed a field. *Did I leave home only to recreate the exact same thing here?*

nine

The last rays of sunlight dimmed as Meredith hit the edge of Abrams's claim. "See? We made it."

Tucker gave her an exasperated look. "If you say, 'I told you so,' I'll push you in the river."

"No, you wouldn't. I'd push you in first because I've listened to an endless string of grumpy mutterings all day."

"You'd have to fight an army of mosquitoes to get close enough to make good on that threat." He batted away a buzzing insect.

"They are thicker this year." Meredith readjusted a strap on the knapsack she wore. "Hello! We're back!"

"It's about time." Old Abrams popped into view. "Rafferty over there's been holdin' off on supper until you took a mind to show up. I'm about to suffer a sinking spell from hunger."

"We can't have that!"

Abrams waited until they came abreast of him. He lowered his voice and leaned closer. "One of you better talk sense into Ian Rafferty. He's whilin' away his time with foolish pursuits. At this rate, come spring of next year, he won't have more'n a pinch of gold dust. He'll have to slink back home with his tail betwixt his legs 'cuz he can't afford grub for the next year."

"He's a grown man," Tucker grumbled. "He can do what he likes."

"Once you see what he's been up to, you'll think nutty old Clemment's downright sane by comparison."

The man on the other side of Ian's claim displayed a wide array of peculiarities. Meredith couldn't imagine what Ian

71

could possibly do to earn such a comparison. Instead of saying anything, she headed for the bridge. Knowing she'd reach the other side of the roiling river without any effort convinced her Ian Rafferty was clever, not crazy.

"Welcome back!" Ian walked over and immediately took the knapsack off her back.

"Careful! I have eggs in the top."

Ian inclined his head to acknowledge her warning. "I'll help Tucker unload everything. Abrams, why don't you dish up supper?"

Weary as she felt, Meredith stepped into her cabin and almost wept with gratitude. Ian had started a fire so the house would be warm—but better still, he'd filled the galvanized tub with water and left it on the hearth. She'd just wash her hands and face now, but as soon as she finished supper, she'd come and spoil herself with a good, long soak.

"Did Bess behave herself?"

"Never thought I'd like a mule," Tucker confessed, "but she was a godsend."

The men dropped off the knapsacks and went back outside to unload the provisions. It would take at least two more trips to carry in everything they'd need for the next winter—but each bag of beans and every pound of flour testified to God's faithfulness.

"Sis," Tucker said as he plopped down the last parcel, "don't bother arranging everything. I'm starving, and if we don't hurry over, Abrams is going to drink all of the coffee."

Meredith laughed. "Is it hunger or coffee that's driving you?"

"Both."

Moments later, Meredith knocked on Ian's door. He walked up from behind her. "Go on in. My home's always open to you."

She and Tucker went inside. Four crates surrounded a cot. What had once been the base of a sled lay across the cot, turning it into a table.

Abrams thumped the speckled coffeepot in the center. "Chow's on. Grace better be short, 'cuz I've waited to eat longer than a man ought to."

Too hungry and tired to be sociable, she and Tucker sank onto the crates. They listened as Ian thanked the Lord for granting them traveling mercies and providing for the meal, then started eating. Very little conversation flowed. Once the meal ended and the coffeepot was emptied, Ian looked at Abrams. "Ready?"

"Sure." Abrams rose from the table and carried the lamp out the door, leaving them with the light of a single candle.

Ian waited a moment, then urged, "Turn around."

Her skirts tangled and snagged on the rough crate. Meredith carefully disentangled herself and pivoted. Her breath caught in her throat.

☙

"It's beautiful!"

The lamp Abrams held outside filtered through an assortment of bottles.

"That," Tucker's tone echoed with wry disbelief, "is undoubtedly the strangest window I've ever seen."

"Stained glass. You made a stained-glass window." Meredith could scarcely speak in more than a reverent whisper. She walked toward it. Her forefinger hovering a mere inch above the open bottles' mouths, she traced the dark cross that deep brown bottles formed in the center.

"Well?" Abrams hollered. "Do they like it?"

"My sister is captivated." Tucker started talking to Ian about heat loss.

Ian answered back about thick mortar between the bottles

and the air trapped inside them.

The precise content of their conversation didn't matter to Meredith. Her cabin had one window just large enough for them to squeeze out of in case of a fire or something blocking the door. All winter long, shutters and a tightly nailed length of leather closed off that window. The notion of having a sliver of light or color enthralled her.

The light behind the window faded. Abrams stomped back in. "It's purdier from the outside. Leastways, it is after dark. Makes me regret not keeping them bottles for myself."

Meredith took in the pattern of color Ian used: green, blue, and brown bottles alternated around the outside, amber ones formed the next row all the way around, then the entire center was clear with the exception of rectangular and square brown bottles that formed the cross. "Just imagine waking to this."

"Had I known how much you'd like it, I would have made mine half that size so you could have one, too." Ian motioned toward a few odd bottles lined up on the floor directly beneath the window. "You're welcome to have those as a start."

Meredith stooped down and frowned. "Oh, Mr. Abrams. I recognize this bottle. It's Positive Rheumatic Cure. My mother, bless her soul, used it."

"Folks don't know how bad the rheumatiz gets. 'Specially in the winter. I'm gonna have to load up on the cure. Ran out last month."

"We would have brought back a bottle for you."

The old man patted her cheek. "Darlin', you put me in mind of my daughter. Violet's got that same streak of kindness."

"You have a daughter?" Tucker blurted out.

"Yup. I'm gonna go back home to her soon as I strike it rich." He shuffled uncomfortably. "Well, I'm going on over to my cabin now."

"Tomorrow is Sunday." Ian leaned against the wall right

next to the window. "Will you be worshipping with us?"

"And having Sunday supper?" Meredith tacked on.

"Nah. Gotta make up for lost time."

Ian and Tucker didn't say anything, but they each took an oil lamp and stood by the riverbank as Abrams crossed the bridge. They knew he couldn't swim and was too proud to confess he was afraid of falling in. Meredith watched as they stood like sentinels, keeping watch—two strong men who wouldn't have hesitated a heartbeat about jumping into the frigid, fast-moving current to rescue a peculiar, grumpy old man. The sight didn't frighten her in the least. She had every confidence in them and believed that God would let no ill befall them.

Waves of weariness washed over her as the men turned and approached her. Meredith didn't want to confess how exhausted she'd grown from the muddy ten-mile trek from town. Instead, she went back into Ian's cabin and started clearing the table.

"Leave that," he ordered. "I have one last thing to show you ere you go home."

Meredith and Tucker accompanied him around the cabin, past the plowed field, and toward the stand of trees. She kept looking down, trying to avoid tripping over a stone or a rut.

"Well?" Ian sounded jubilant. "What do you think?"

Tucker started laughing.

Delighted, Meredith looked at her twin. Twice now, Ian had gotten him to laugh. Tucker reached over and turned her head to the side so she could see what tickled him.

Ian swept his hand in a gesture that would do a snake-oil charlatan proud. "Only the best for those who want the comforts of home."

Meredith's jaw dropped.

ten

Meredith slipped from the outhouse early the next morning, unsure whether to be sheepish or delighted. A lady didn't discuss such topics, but she couldn't help wanting to thank Ian again. And again. And again.

Just to keep from flinging her arms around Ian in thanks last night, she'd clung to Tucker's arm and babbled in delight. She'd probably made a complete fool of herself, but Ian was far too polite to say so. She'd finally stammered something and run back home to soak in the bath. She didn't take as long as she wanted to. Tucker had to be tired, too, and she wanted him to enjoy hot water. She'd no more than lain down when she heard him come into the cabin. A mere breath later, she'd fallen fast asleep.

"Ian wants to know if you want to worship here or over at his place."

"Do you mind if it's at his place? The light shining through that window would be perfect."

"Okay. Ian invited Abrams again, but that ornery old man won't come. I'm going to go see if Mr. Clemment is interested."

Tucker coaxed Mr. Clemment to come over and worship with them. Mr. Clemment arrived in overalls that he wore backwards. He looked slightly confused and grew wary as Tucker introduced him to Ian.

Ian slowly extended his right hand. "I'm glad to meet the neighbor on the other side of that fine bramble that separates our claims."

"God never made a better bramble!" Suddenly, Mr. Clemment warmed up to Ian and started telling him all of the varieties of birds that would peck the berries.

Ian listened and asked a few questions. Treating the odd man with respect, he managed to steer him into the house and seated him beside Meredith. " 'Tis grand to have neighbors worship together, isn't it?"

Meredith patted Mr. Clemment's hand. "We're glad you came."

Ian reached over and took his Bible from the table. Meredith watched her twin. When they'd gone to the mercantile, she'd seen Tucker longingly running his fingers over the cover of a Bible. He'd not picked it up, though. Since Ian shared his Bible, they could do without buying one for themselves. Even though that was the case, Meredith knew her brother missed having a complete Bible every bit as much as she did.

"Tucker, here." Ian handed his Bible to Tucker. "Why don't you read to us from the Word of God today?"

Tucker accepted the Bible, sat down, and reverently rested his hand atop the leather cover for a long moment before opening the pages.

Meredith looked from her brother's hands to Ian as he sat on a crate. Ian's kindness and generosity and Tucker's reverence stirred her heart.

After Tucker read from the Psalms, each of them took turns speaking of the Lord's goodness. Ian ended with a prayer. Although an altogether simple service, observing the Lord's Day still felt good.

Tired as she'd been from travel, Meredith decided beans would make for an easy and filling meal—especially since she had eggs. One precious egg allowed her to make a pan of cornbread.

After Sunday supper, Mr. Clemment paced around the garden plot. "I like sunflower seeds. Are you planting sunflowers?"

"No, they don't have sufficient season to grow up here." Ian proceeded to explain the crops they planned.

"Oh!" Meredith perked up. "Socks is going to send to Sitka for free seeds for us. They ought to come in a week. The only seeds he had were for parsnips, so I took a packet."

"Been a long, long while since I had parsnip soup." Mr. Clemment scratched his side. "Don't suppose you've got a recipe for it."

"I do. Once we have a nice crop of parsnips, I'll be sure to make soup for Sunday supper especially for you."

"Hold on, Sis." Tucker gave her a warning look. "You can't go counting your chickens before they hatch."

"Chickens are fine birds," Clemment said.

Meredith didn't want to be rude, so she nodded acknowledgment to Mr. Clemment. "Tucker, we live by faith."

"Not by faith alone. You have to face facts, too. Life brings hardships and trials. No matter how hard you and Ian work in that garden, you can't count on anything coming of it."

"Just like prospecting," Clemment agreed. "You can work your fingers to the bone and hardly get a thing for all your efforts."

"Don't be faulting the lass for her bright outlook. Naysayers never get anything started and done. Her cheerful attitude is a wondrous thing." A slow smile tugged at the corner of Ian's mouth. "I'm thinking your mother named you well. A merrier woman I'll never meet."

"Mama called me Merry when I was small."

The smile broke across Ian's face. "And with your leave, I'll call you the same. 'Tis a fitting name indeed for you."

Delight rippled through her. "Please feel free to."

"Good. Merry you are, so 'tis Merry you'll be."

❧

"Merry?"

She ceased planting lettuce seeds, sat back on her heels, and faced Ian. "Yes?"

"You've mentioned your mother a few times. Tucker said she's passed on. What about your father?"

She looked away and rasped, "He's no longer with us."

"Ahh." He stretched out the sound in such a way that it carried the flavor of sorrow, as well as understanding. "I apologize. I didn't mean to add to your grief."

She bowed her head and covered the infinitesimal seeds with a fine layer of soil. The first batch of lettuce was starting to mature. By staggering the planting, they'd stretch the time they'd be able to enjoy the produce. Merry tried to concentrate on her task, but she worried the way her hand shook would tell Ian how much he'd rattled her composure.

Why did I ever promise Tucker I wouldn't tell anyone? Keeping the secret is so hard. I feel like I'm lying or dancing around the truth. Ian is such a good man, yet we're repaying his generosity and kindness with deceit. Meredith swallowed to dislodge the thick ball in her throat, but it didn't help.

Silence hung between them. The song of birds didn't begin to cover the awkwardness.

"I won't mention him again, Merry. I can see how much I've upset you, and I'm truly sorry."

Tears blurred her vision as guilt mounted. Unable to speak, Meredith merely nodded.

Ian continued to work. The steady sound of his hoe made it easy for Meredith to know precisely where he was. He'd moved down that row and now came back toward her. Normally, they'd carry on a comfortable conversation while working in the garden. The strain of the silence pulled at her conscience. Bound by her promise to Tucker, she couldn't say anything—but the topic weighed so heavily on her heart, nothing else came to mind.

The sharp sound of a slap made her look up. Ian frowned while looking at his forearm. "I've seen hummingbirds smaller than the mosquitoes around here!"

"Tucker says that Alaskan mosquitoes must not have heard the rule that everything is supposed to be bigger in Texas."

"I'm sure the onions in Texas are larger. The few that did grow certainly weren't worth the effort."

"I'm not so sure about the parsnips, either. Mr. Clemment will be so disappointed if we don't succeed with them."

He leaned on his hoe. "Do you think the parsnips are actually normal in size? I'm thinking that the carrots, potatoes, and parsnips will be ordinary, but the long, long daylight hours are making things above the ground grow huge. Anything by comparison would look meager."

"I hadn't thought about that." She scanned the garden. Calling it a garden seemed ludicrous. Early on, they'd had to thin the vegetables. Instead of tossing aside anything, Ian decided it would be good stewardship to plow a few more rows and transplant anything they thinned. But he'd had to do a few more rows. . .and a few more again.

Miners who'd paid Meredith to do their laundry and mending last year came by again. One look at the garden, and they'd eagerly bartered for vegetables. The funds from those first transactions paid for canning jars and more buttons.

Meredith and Tucker had come to an agreement: any of the money or goods she earned with laundry, sewing, and the garden would go toward their own needs. Tucker didn't want any of that to go toward repaying everyone back in Texas. He, alone, would do that with whatever gold they mined.

"Aha!"

Ian's sound made Meredith jump. She gave him a startled look.

"You think my question holds a grain of truth. Much as I love potatoes—and what self-respecting Irishman wouldn't?— 'tis a crying shame that they don't grow so big here. But I'm thinking we'll have enough to get us through the winter. Don't you?"

She looked at that area of the patch. "I'm not so sure. . . not if I roast those two hares you snared today. Potatoes and carrots and roast. . ."

Ian looked up at the sky, then heaved a sigh. "How am I to know when 'tis suppertime? The notion of living with the midnight sun sounded novel when first I came. But now I can't sleep worth a hoot and don't know when 'tis mealtime."

"Time doesn't have much meaning up here. If you're having trouble sleeping, you can hang something dark in front of the windows and by the door. That helps."

"I drove nails into the log directly above my window last night. Knotted the corners of a brown blanket 'round the nails."

"Good."

"Not so good. Just as I was finally falling asleep, one end slid off and pulled the other down with it. I gave up and put the blanket over my head—but then I could scarcely breathe and started roasting."

"Oh dear."

His mouth formed a self-deprecating smile. "I'd call myself a pathetic wretch, but I'd be lying. Just one look around, and I can see how blessed I am. I've a claim, a garden, and godly neighbors. What more could a man ask for?"

For his godly neighbors to be forthright instead of putting up pretenses. The answer shot through her mind. Unable to face him any longer, Meredith rose to her feet and dusted off her hands as she walked to the water bucket. Sipping water from the dipper, she fought to regain her composure.

"Hey!" A pair of men appeared on the edge of the woods. "Didn't think it was possible a woman was round these parts, but Matthews said we'd find one here—and there you are!"

Ian appeared at her side in an instant. "Did you men need something?"

"Heard tell the gal takes in laundry and mending."

"She might." Ian's voice sounded controlled and quiet, but at the same time, those two clipped words made it clear he wouldn't put up with any nonsense.

The men drew closer. "Now that winter's over, we've got clothes that need washing." One raked his fingers through his greasy hair and beard. "A haircut would suit me fine. A shave, too."

Meredith shook her head.

"The lady's not a barber." Ian stayed close and murmured, "If you don't want to do their laundry, put your hand in the pocket of your apron. If you'll do it, slip your hand into mine."

Every bit of money she could earn mattered. Meredith slid her hand into Ian's rough, warm palm. His fingers closed about hers. He squeezed gently, and Meredith struggled to stay composed.

I'm living a lie, and he's protecting me.

"Well, that answers that," one told the other.

"What?" Ian half growled.

"Heard the gal was here with her brother. That feller over yonder looks like her. He's gotta be her kin. Kinda hoped she'd take a shine to one of us and marry up. Guess you beat us to her."

"Crying shame, too. She's pretty."

Ian didn't look at her. He simply stepped forward and

tucked her behind himself.

"We ain't meanin' to insult you or scare your missus," the other said to Ian. "Havin' a wife to do the laundry and cookin'—well, you're set real fine. Us? We just need some stuff done."

Ian didn't budge. "Women are worth far more than just being laundresses. This woman, in particular."

"You're right. Betcha she's a fine cook, too."

Meredith could feel the way Ian bristled at their comments. Whenever bachelors happened by, they invariably proposed. They wanted a woman to cook their meals, tend their clothes, and warm their bed. Even Mr. Abrams and Mr. Clemment had suggested marriage. Ian, alone, bore the distinction of being the only man she'd seen in the past fifteen months who hadn't asked for her hand.

Does he have a wife or sweetheart back home? Or does he think I'm as attractive as last week's fish?

"How much laundry do you have, and what kind of mending?"

He remembered me asking those same questions of Mr. Abrams. She stood on tiptoe and peeped over Ian's shoulder.

"Two pair of britches and two shirts apiece. Most everything's short a button or two."

Elbowing his companion, the other jerked his head toward the garden and moaned. "Matthews was right. They've got fresh truck. Lots of it!"

Tucker sauntered over. His hooded expression wouldn't allow the strangers to know what he was thinking, but Meredith knew full well he noticed Ian's protective stance. "What's going on?"

"We're looking to have some laundry and mending done and to buy up some of those greens you folks are growing."

Ian turned to Tucker. "Meredith's planning to can any of

the green beans and wax beans we don't eat fresh."

"You got all season to grow more. Surely you could spare us some now. And some lettuce, too. That's lettuce, isn't it?"

The man had good call to wonder. Ian had never seen lettuce even half that size. "Aye, it's lettuce. And beside it— that's cabbage."

The two men whispered to each other. One finally cleared his throat. "One buck, cash money, and a pinch of gold dust. We get two quarts of fresh beans, two quart jars of beans the gal's put up, two heads of cabbage, and two heads of lettuce, and the lady does our laundry and mending."

Ian snorted.

"Two bucks."

After supper one night a few weeks back, she, Tucker, and Ian had come to an agreement regarding the price of their goods. For the effort they put into the garden, they needed to make a profit. After all, it did take away from the time Ian would prospect. But the money earned would also be a fine way of making it so others wouldn't realize they'd found that sliver of a gold vein. Even so, if any of the three of them felt led to sell at a reduced rate or even give away food to someone in need, that would be fine.

Ian and Tucker exchanged a stern look. Then Tucker looked at her. Ian still didn't budge—he kept her directly behind himself, out of their view. Something in the way the strangers acted didn't put Meredith in a generous frame of mind. She gave her head a slight shake.

"The mercantile in Goose Chase charges a buck and a half for hamburger steak and onion in a can," Tucker said. "One stinking can for a buck fifty. I don't doubt they'd pay that much for a head of cabbage."

"Probably pay us that much and charge a customer more," Ian chimed in.

"The three of you can't eat all that," one of the men wheedled. "It'll just go to waste."

Merry slipped from behind Ian and stood between him and her brother. "I'll just slice up any extra cabbage and whip up batches of sauerkraut. It'll keep in crocks for months on end."

"Other men are eager to buy our excess, and for fair prices." Ian stared at the men. "But those men also understand the value of having a lady do their laundry and mending. Bad enough, you've offered gracious little for the food, but I'll not stand by and let you insult Meredith. It would be best if you went off and struck a deal with someone else."

"We can't do that. There aren't any other women, and no one else planted a garden."

"You should have thought about those things before you made such a paltry offer." Tucker made a shooing motion. "Go on and get off my land."

"Six bucks!"

Ian folded his arms across his chest. "No. You insulted the lady. She'll not be lowering herself to wash your clothes at any price."

"Then five bucks. Forget the laundry or mending. We'll pay you five bucks, cash money, and you give us two heads of lettuce and two heads of cabbage and—"

"No more," Tucker ground out.

"My brother means to say," Meredith blurted out, "we'll agree to five dollars for the items you just specified." She felt sure her brother was going to send the men packing even though they'd offered an exorbitant sum.

"Deal!" One of the men scrambled over.

"But you don't come back. Ever." Tucker stared at them.

After they left, Tucker ignored her. He looked at Ian. "I don't care how much they offer. Sis isn't doing their laundry or mending. Ever."

"I agree. And they'll not buy another morsel of food."

"Are you going to bother to ask me?"

"No," they said in unison.

She huffed. "I have a mind of my own."

"Aye, you do. And a sound mind it is." Ian then tacked on "But you've also a tender heart. What kind of men would we be to stand by and let anyone abuse your helpfulness or hurt your feelings?"

"My feelings aren't hurt."

Ian shook his head. "Lass, that just proves our point. You've forgiven those louts already. Fact is, they didn't care about your feelings. They had sufficient money to make a fair offer. They had no honor. Never deal with someone who lacks integrity."

For the rest of the day, while the men used pickaxes and the sledgehammer to chip deeper into the stony earth, Ian's words pounded into Meredith's mind over and over again. *"Never deal with someone who lacks integrity."* How would Ian feel when he learned the truth?

eleven

"Thanks." Ian accepted the dipper of water from Meredith and took a long, refreshing gulp. Tucker had loaded Bess with garden truck and led her to town. Several more trips would be essential—both to sell the produce and to bring in supplies for the coming year.

Meredith accepted the empty dipper. "Thank you for sending Tucker to town today. He can be so stubborn!"

Ian grimaced. "Aye. But that thumb has to be paining him something awful."

She nodded. "He knows better than to be using a wet sledgehammer on a rainy day. He's lucky lightning didn't strike him."

"I'd be a hypocrite to condemn him for that. We get so much rain, there aren't many days' work we'd get done if we ran inside each time the sky took a mind to spit."

"I wonder how far he'll get before someone stops him and asks to buy something straight off Bess."

"Not far." Ian lifted his pickax. "I knotted everything on with a diamond hitch, so he'll be able to take things off without her losing balance as long as he keeps the sides fairly even."

"That's good."

"Best you know, Merry, that the vein in the stone isn't getting any wider yet. We'd hoped it would grow big and fat."

"It still might. Even if it doesn't, you're getting more than we ever panned."

"I saw you panning yesterday."

"Why not? I was waiting for the laundry pot to boil. I go about a pinch and a half of gold dust. With gold at sixteen dollars per ounce, that's not a bad show for an afternoon's work."

"Pure gold is sixteen dollars per ounce, Merry. Gold dust is impure. When it's all melted and the dross is removed, it weighs far less."

"Oh."

The disappointment on her face tugged at his heart. "Every bit counts."

"Yes, it does." She smiled. "Did Tucker speak to you about removing rock now in as much bulk as possible?"

"He did." Ian found a comfortable grip on the pickax. "I'm in full agreement. We'll be able to crush it down and put it through the shaker box during the worst of the winter."

"So you don't mind?"

"Why would I mind?" He gave her a surprised look. "Long days like this can allow us extreme amounts of outdoor work. When we're locked inside by the most frigid part of the winter, we'll still be able to make progress."

"It'll make a mess of your cabin—all the dust and grit."

"Man came from dust and will return to dust."

Merry's laughter filled the air. "Woman came from bone. Where does that leave her?"

"If all goes as God intended, it leaves her right by her man's side and inside his heart." *And that's where I'd like you to be.*

"Well, for now, this woman is going to do a few chores. Tucker said he'll be back tonight, but I'm not so sure."

"I believe he will. The sunlight will allow him to travel safely, and he's got a lot of stamina."

"That's true." Her pretty hazel eyes sparkled. "I think it's more a matter of stubbornness. Once my brother sets his mind to something, he pursues it with a singleness of mind that is nearly unshakable."

"Old Abrams said something to that effect last night." Ian remembered the old man's bluster. "Only he wound up calling your twin a thickheaded bulldog."

The matter neither of them addressed was glaring: Until now, Meredith and Ian hadn't been alone. She'd gone to town with Tucker on the other trip. His leaving her behind and in Ian's safekeeping showed a measure of trust that Ian understood. He planned to be worthy of that trust. Clenching the pickax helped him do just that. Otherwise, he'd cave in to temptation, grab Meredith, and help himself to a sweet, sweet kiss.

"Anything special you'd like for supper?"

He stopped. "You needn't cook for me, Merry. I've put beans to soak. I can boil them later."

"It's no trouble, Ian. I don't mind."

"I do, though. Our bargain ended. You have no call to cook for me."

Resting her hands on her hips, Merry gave him an exasperated look. "That deal? Don't be ridiculous. You've been sharing your food far longer than we agreed to, and you've plowed more than twice what we agreed upon."

"You've helped weed, thin, and transplant." He readjusted his hold on the pickax. "Add to that all the beans you've canned."

"In jars you bought." She stooped down and pleaded, "Ian, let's not haggle. Please let me cook. You have every reason and right to claim the gold here."

"No, lass, I don't. The Lord was present when we made our agreement. He knew where the riches lay—and He had Tucker see them first. The believers in the Bible worked together and shared all they had in common. Tucker and you are working every bit as hard as I am. I couldn't face myself in the mirror or my Maker on Judgment Day if I hoarded this for myself."

"You're being honorable." Tears shimmered in her eyes. "How, then, can you want us to partake in your blessings and refuse to accept what we have to offer? From now on, I'm making the meals."

He shook his head. Every morning of his life, he'd seen Da give Ma a good-morning kiss, and she'd give him another as he left for the fields. Since the day Braden and Maggie married, they'd taken up that same tradition. *If I sit across the breakfast table from this woman, I'll long for that same closeness.* Refusing her offer would hurt her, though. In a voice every bit as rough as the gravel he was creating, Ian said, "Midday and supper. I make my own breakfasts."

The smile on her face made him glad he'd compromised. She rose with grace and went off to see to her chores.

Ian chipped away at the ground. The pickax did a fair job, but sinking a hole into anything took a lot of effort. Even though it was summer and sunlight ruled both day and night, the glacial rock didn't care. As long as Ian worked, he kept warm. After a few minutes of stopping and talking, the insidious cold started making his muscles knot.

Spying a small offshoot of gold, Ian wanted to significantly widen the area they'd begun to dig. He established a rhythm and kept at it.

"Ian!"

Merry's voice brought him to a halt. "Are you ready to eat?"

"I'm always ready to eat." He set down the pickax and hopped out of the hole. A quick backward glance made him say, "It looks like I'm digging a grave."

Merry shivered. "Don't say that!"

"Oh, lass, I'm sorry. I wasn't thinking." Recriminations ran through his mind. Grief still held great sway over her—so much that she couldn't bear to mention her father. *I have to mind my tongue. That was a terrible slip.*

"Never mind." The blithe tone she used didn't take away the sadness in her eyes.

They sat on crates over by the river to eat. "I'll never tire of this view." Ian watched as the water bubbled and whooshed by. "The sight and sound are lovely indeed."

"It's pretty in winter, too. Because we came from Texas, I'd never lived with snow before."

"I'd think the novelty would wear off once the cold sets in."

"Boredom is just as big an enemy as cold. Tucker's suggestion of taking rocks inside to pulverize and extract the gold—it's his way of staying busy. He spent two solid weeks last winter weaving us snowshoes."

"This winter, we can draw a board on wood or cloth and use rocks to make a game of draughts."

"We did that." The corners of Meredith's mouth twitched. "But that game grows tedious. Tucker came up with a different use for those rocks. He nearly drove me to distraction trying to learn to juggle them."

"Did he, now?"

Meredith shook her head. "Not really. He never did manage to keep three in the air. They'd fall somewhere, and he'd scoop up more. He wouldn't give up until he'd used up all the stones and they peppered the beds and floor."

"That's a man acting out of desperation. What did you do to keep busy?"

Laughter bubbled out of her. "I dodged stones."

After his laughter died down, Ian said, "You're a delightful lass, Merry Smith."

"Look at the two of you," Abrams groused loudly.

Ian bristled at the old man's intrusion. Having just paid Merry a compliment, he wanted to follow up and say something more.

"Coulda invited me to lunch," Abrams continued on. "Since

Tucker went to town, the bridge is spanning the river."

"But the bread I'm baking won't be ready until supper." Meredith stood. "Wouldn't you rather come tonight?"

"Now that's more like it! What else are you fixin'?"

"Why did you waste your breath to ask?" Ian slapped his hat on his head. "You know whatever Merry makes will be far better than anything you or I would rustle up."

Abrams shouted back, "I'm a better cook than you, Rafferty!"

"That's not saying much. Anyone's a better cook than I am."

"You more than make up for that lack with your farming and hunting." A pale pink suffused Meredith's cheeks. She swiped Ian's plate from his hands and walked away.

Ian fought the urge to dash after her. Instead, he made a quick round of the snares he'd set. Every last one lay empty. *Lord, You know I'm falling in love with Merry. You own the cattle on a thousand hills. I'm not asking for a fatted calf, though. Couldn't You please see fit to fill my snares with a couple of hare or grouse? Don't let her confidence in me dwindle. She's always had Tucker to lean on. He's a fine man, Lord, but if Merry becomes my wife, she needs to see me as the one who can provide for her.*

"Ian?"

≥≥

"Ian?" Meredith called again as she walked around a stump. Spying him, she changed direction toward him.

He shot to his feet.

She glanced at the empty snare. Methodical as he was, she knew this would be the last one he'd check. Ian always went in a clockwise sweep of the traps and snares. His hands hung empty at his sides. "I know how important it is for you to be prospecting. Just because I said you're a good hunter, please don't feel I wanted you to bring in supper tonight."

"Sad fact is, nothing's caught yet."

"I was afraid of that—oh! Not that there wouldn't be anything. That you'd feel obligated to bring in the meat. We have a fair store of smoked fish, and I made several jars of confit with the squirrels you've gotten. I'll come up with something."

"We've hours to go before suppertime." His voice sounded strained. "I'll check the snares in a few hours."

"All right." She looked down at the dusty hem of her dress, then back at him. "The salad and bread are wonderful additions to our table, and we're thankful for each bite. Please don't think there's anything wrong with a plate of beans."

"Are you reminding me to be thankful for whatever we have?"

"If that's so, it's unintentional. I wanted to let you know that *I'm* thankful. Tucker and I are eating better now than we have since we came up here." As soon as she spoke, Meredith wanted to take back those words. "I didn't mean that the way it sounded. Tucker works hard, and we've done just fine."

"Your brother is a good man." Ian gave a definitive nod. "Hardworking, God-fearing, and he loves you."

Tension draining out of her, Meredith grinned. "Almost as much as I love him."

"I hold no doubt that he'd disagree." Ian dusted off his hands. "You're a rare woman."

Pleasure thrummed through her. "Thank you. That's kind of you to say."

"I'm not just saying it. I'm meaning it." He cast a look around them. "Since I've arrived, I've seen any number of miners tromp over here. You sew and do laundry and write letters for them. Every last one has spoken of marriage to you."

Her jaw dropped.

"Before you think I've eavesdropped, a handful have proposed to you in my presence, and Tucker told me the rest have done likewise. Know this, Meredith Smith: I'm speaking from an earnest heart, not out of flattery in hopes of gaining a wife to wash and mend my clothes."

"Oh." She wasn't sure what more to say.

"I'd best get back to work."

"Me, too." She watched him stride over to the smokehouse, hop down into the hole in the earth he'd been digging, and take up his pickax. *So he's not attracted to me. Ian's the first man I've met in Alaska who appeals to me, and he doesn't even want a wife.*

twelve

I did it. I finally told Merry I'm courting her. The way those strange men dump filthy, stinking clothes at her feet and ask her to be their wife—it shows no respect or caring. A huge chunk of rock yielded to the pickax. Thoroughly pleased with himself, Ian kept working. *Now that she knows I appreciate her for her kind heart and lively spirit, she'll understand I'm different.*

He'd work himself to death if necessary to be sure Merry had whatever she needed. To be sure, the lass never wanted much at all, but Ian was determined. He'd hunt and farm so she'd never have to be satisfied with a meager meal, and he'd coax every last fleck of gold from the claim in order to provide for her.

Twice that afternoon, he paused from work only long enough to drink water and check the snares. Empty. They remained empty.

Lord, I'm counting on You. Merry needs to see how I can provide for her.

A gunshot sounded.

Ian leapt from the hole and snatched the shotgun he always kept within reach. "Merry, get in the cabin!"

"Git offa my claim!" Mr. Abrams shouted.

Instead of obeying Ian, Meredith came running toward him. Ian turned toward Abrams's claim and shoved Meredith behind his back.

"Settle down, you old geezer." A man stood in the middle of Abrams's claim. He held two huge salmon. "I'm fixin' to trade. Feller named Smith sent me."

"What do I get? You're on my property."

Meredith popped out from behind Ian. "Why, Mr. Abrams, letting him cross your property is your contribution to our supper tonight."

"Merry, get back behind me." Ian didn't wait for her to comply. He stepped in front of her.

"I'm in no danger." She started to shift.

Ian kept hold of his shotgun and reached back with his other hand. He grabbed her and held her in place. "Abrams has that rifle in his arms. There's no telling what he'll shoot, but it's not going to be you."

"Rafferty, what do you say?" Abrams shouted.

"Put down your rifle and let him come across."

Abrams shook his head. "Dunno. Bears like salmon. Might be one takes a mind to follow this man. Can't let down my guard."

The stranger pushed past Abrams. "A bear would want the salmon, not you, you old goat."

Meredith muffled a giggle.

As the man started across the bridge, Tucker glanced at her. "You like salmon."

"I adore it."

"It's written all over your face. One look, and he'll know he has the advantage on this barter. Go on inside. I promise, you'll have salmon for supper."

To his relief, Meredith walked to her cabin and went inside. He didn't want men ogling her. Once she shut the door, Ian folded his arms across his chest and waited. Whoever spoke first in a bargain always walked away with the shorter end of the deal. Meredith wanted salmon, and Ian determined he would strike a bargain whereby she'd get both of the ones this man carried.

"Coffee," the man said as he stepped off the bridge, onto the shore.

"Coffee," Ian repeated, surprised Tucker would have sent anyone to trade fish for his beloved drink.

The man nodded. "Erik Kauffey. Sounds like the drink, but spelled different. I brought these to barter. You've got to admit, they're beauts. Big ones, too."

"I'm Ian Rafferty. Smith's my partner." He motioned toward a stump. "Set those down over there."

"Where'd the little lady go?"

Ian gave him a steely glare. "Did you come here to barter or to banter?"

Kauffey heaved a so-that's-the-way-things-go sigh. "The salmon were fresh caught this morning. One's female, so you'll even be getting roe in the bargain."

"Never could stand the stuff." Clearly, Kauffey accepted that Meredith was off-limits, so he pursued the barter by pointing out the advantages of Ian's obtaining the salmon. Ian knew better than to jump in and agree, so he shrugged. "I've heard roe makes for good fertilizer."

"Roe's good to bait snares for birds. Lots of ptarmigan here."

"Ptarmigan. They're in the grouse family, right?"

"Yeah. White-tailed ones are local. Wings are always white, but come snow season, they're all white. Good eating." Kauffey sauntered over toward the vegetable garden.

"I haven't seen many."

"Funny birds, ptarmigan." Kauffey headed toward the far corner. "They show up and disappear in a wink. You ought to be glad they haven't been around much. They'd eat every last leaf you have here."

"They'd have to fight the hares for the privilege."

Kauffey squatted down and inspected a head of lettuce. "If you take it into consideration, I'm not averse to taking something if a rabbit or bird took the first bite."

"I'm sure we can work something out."

Ten minutes later, Meredith exited her cabin and met Ian over by the stump. "That man practically danced across the bridge to go home."

Ian grinned. "You know those two heads of lettuce and the cabbage that the hares nibbled? He took all three and I tossed in some rhubarb. The way he dashed off, I think he was afraid I'd change my mind."

"Up close, these salmon are even bigger than I thought. A quarter of one will be a feast for us. I can smoke the rest. Oh! If I put some of it in a pail and tuck it in the cleft of that rock over there, the water will keep it chilled. We can enjoy fresh salmon again tomorrow!"

"That's clever of you." He pulled his knife from his belt sheath. "I'll—"

"You'll let me see to them. With Tucker loving to fish, I'm a dab hand at this. You have more important things to do."

"Like what?"

"Put in a fireplace."

"I've decided to put in a stove."

She reared back. "A stove? How will you ever get a stove?"

"I know Socks has one in his mercantile for thirty-two dollars. 'Tis highway robbery. But shipping one from Oregon to here will be reasonable."

"I—I didn't mean the cost." Hectic color filled her cheeks. "I wondered how you'd transport it. Wily's umiak would sink the minute you loaded the stove aboard."

"Wagon wheels. By affixing axels and wheels to the box, I can have Bess pull it in."

"You're serious!"

"That I am. Sears won't ship to Alaska, but the catalog shows a Southern Sunshine cookstove. It's a dandy thing. My folks will find one and ship it here. I figure the crate it comes in can serve as a wagon of sorts. It'll be easier to haul produce into Goose Chase."

"Are you sure you want to sell Bess when the weather changes?"

"There's insufficient feed for her here. I just wanted to mention about the wagon so if there was anything heavy or bulky that you and Tucker might want, you could take advantage of the opportunity."

"Thank you. We'll keep it in mind."

Something in her tone of voice struck him as odd. Ian cleared his throat. "Forgive me if I'm out of place, but it occurs to me that Tucker is your only family. My family back in Oregon would be more than willing to locate goods and ship them for you. It's far cheaper."

"That's a kind offer. Tucker and I actually have an uncle, but we already have everything we need."

Ian didn't challenge her. To his way of thinking, Meredith didn't have half of what she needed.

Over the next two months, he grew increasingly perplexed at why she and Tucker bought only the barest essentials for themselves. It made no sense; the garden flourished and brought cash, gold dust, and a wide variety of items in barter—not enough to make them all rich, but certainly sufficient to provide comfortably for their needs.

Perhaps they're worried next year will be harsh and they're trying to set aside for lean times—like Joseph advised Pharaoh to do. With that in mind, Ian determined to work even harder to reassure Merry that she'd not have to worry.

❧

Merry stretched as Tucker twisted from side to side. Ian emerged from the smokehouse. "All done?" he asked.

"Yes." She watched as he carefully latched the door shut. "I don't think we could wedge one more thing in there. That mountain sheep was enormous."

"God's provided well."

"You're right." Merry smiled at Ian. He'd gone out hunting and returned with enough meat to get them through much of the winter, yet he didn't boast. "But there's no reason we can't credit that the Lord used you to supply for our needs."

"Hold on a second. Tucker's the one who brought in all the fish."

Tucker shook his head. "Nope. I caught the trout and Dolly Varden, but the salmon—that's your doing. Kauffey must have come here a dozen times to trade for the greens from that garden of yours."

" 'Tis *our* garden." Ian's brows scrunched into a stern line. "Merry's labored in it every bit as much as I have. And though Kauffey caught the salmon, Tucker, you sent him here to barter."

Merry wanted to hug Ian for how he'd turned the conversation. Instead of boasting about his hunting acumen and all of his success, he'd emphasized Tucker's contributions. Tucker already struggled with feeling indebted. The last thing he needed was to face that same burden in his own home.

"With Merry preserving jars and crocks of everything she gets her hands on, we'll be eating like royalty all winter long."

"He's right, Sis. You've gathered at least five times as many berries this year, too."

"We missed strawberry season entirely. Now that we know they can grow up here, I'd love to plant some next year."

Tucker shook his head.

They're probably too expensive. I shouldn't have said anything.

"Without Bess, Ian won't be able to plow the land. This year's garden was great, but you can't count on it again next year."

"Ah, but we will." Ian smiled. "I came to an agreement with Wily. He gets my mule for the cold season; I get her for the warm. If you're of a mind to be farmers with me again next year, I'd be pleased to continue the partnership."

Merry's heart sang at the promise of another season of working side by side in the field with Ian. They'd had wonderful discussions and lively debates and had shared concerns while in the garden. *Maybe next year, he'll feel settled and ready to take a wife.*

"If you don't mind, I'd like to have Bess drag down more wood for the winter."

"I'm happy to help you down a few trees."

"Wait!" Merry backed up. "Don't you dare start haggling and making another deal. At least not in front of me."

The men exchanged a baffled look.

"The way the two of you wrangle, it's a marvel someone's firstborn child isn't already named."

Eyes twinkling, Ian turned to Tucker. "Now there's a fine notion!"

"Something biblical," Tucker mused. "I always liked Amminadab. That, or Ahaseurus."

"Methuselah's got a nice ring to it."

"You can't do that!"

Tucker crooked a brow. "Give me a couple of good reasons why not."

Feeling a tad sassy, she proclaimed, "Since we don't have the Old Testament, you wouldn't spell it right."

"That's not a problem." Ian stood beside Tucker and smiled like a rascal. "We already have an agreement. You're welcome to borrow my Bible anytime. What kind of man would I be if I went back on my word?"

"Sorry, Sis. You need a better reason."

"All right, I'll give you a great one. Because that poor, defenseless child never did anything to deserve such a terrible fate!"

Ian turned to Tucker. "Don't you think naming a child something like Jehosephat would help him develop character?"

Meredith burst out laughing. "Any son either of you have will already be a character if he takes after you."

"Sis has a point."

"Fine." Ian shrugged. "Then we'll just leave the boys out of the bargain and go for a daughter's name."

thirteen

"That's all mine?" Ian stared in disbelief at the packages, crates, and tins.

"Yup." Socks readjusted his cap. "I need it outta here. Came in three days ago, and I'm already tired of chasing folks away from it. You got stuff there I can't get in. It's makin' my mercantile look bad."

The weather had changed. Ian knew Bess belonged with Wily now. Even with careful packing, she wouldn't be able to carry everything—and Ian didn't want to risk taking her back only to have her freeze or starve because be couldn't get her back to Goose Chase.

Wily leaned against the counter. "By the time January or February comes around, Rafferty, you'll be glad to have all that stuff."

"Probably." Ian stared at the goods his family had sent. He knew they'd really stretched the budget and been incredibly generous. Still, gratitude warred with practicality. He didn't know how he'd get everything to his cabin, and even if he did, he didn't have room in the cabin for all of it. Suddenly, Merry and Tucker's careful and lean planning made a lot more sense.

"Don't worry. I'll help you out." Wily hefted a crate. "It's the least I can do."

It took a lot of consideration and careful balancing, but they managed to load everything into Wily's umiak. "I appreciate this." Ian got aboard and took up a paddle.

Wily settled in, and someone pushed them off. "I reckoned this is as good an excuse as any for me to get a morning of

103

fishing. Probably won't catch anything other than the ague, but you won't hear me complain if I do. I've spent every waking moment of the past three weeks making deliveries. I'll just be glad to have folks leave me be."

It took a lot of effort to row the heavily laden vessel upriver. When they finally reached his claim, Tucker met them at the riverbank. He took a rope and secured the umiak.

"Welcome back." Merry pulled a shawl about her shoulders. "Hello, Wily. How nice to see you, too. I have coffee ready."

Ian didn't want to blink. He'd been gone from Meredith for less than a day, and it felt as if it had been forever. He looked into the sparkling depths of her hazel eyes and knew if that was the only gold he ever found, he'd be the richest man on earth.

"Lookit all that." Abrams traipsed across the bridge.

"Don't bother to ask," Wily snapped. "I didn't bring any spirits."

"I wasn't talkin' to you, you old coot. Ian, got anything there for me?"

"Rafferty's an honorable man. He wouldn't transport whiskey or beer on my umiak."

Ian drew an envelope from his shirt pocket so he could stop the quarrel. "Socks gave me a letter for you."

"It must be from Violet." Merry tucked her hand into the crook of Abrams's arm once he claimed the missive. "I'd love to hear how she's doing."

As they walked off, Wily murmured, "He can't read a lick. Marks an *X* for his signature. Meredith's got such a kind heart, she covers for him."

"Yeah, well, he'll wrangle his way into staying for supper now." Tucker grimaced. "Not only will he drink the entire pot of coffee she has going, he'll bug me until I make another pot after supper."

"If he didn't, I would." Wily shoved a burlap bag into Tucker's hands. "Make yourself useful."

Tucker didn't move. "Rafferty, if there are any bottles in here, I get them. I'm going to put a window in for my sister. Never paid any mind to the color, size, or shape of them 'til now. The blue and the green ones are scarce as hen's teeth. Meredith hasn't said anything, but I know she has her heart set on a pretty window like yours."

"I have absolutely no idea what is in all of this. Once we get inside my cabin, I'll take stock."

Wily barged into Ian's cabin and stopped. "When did you do this?"

"The partition? About a month after the roof went up."

"Doesn't make sense." Wily set down his load. "Why's your bed here with the kitchen stuff instead of in the other room?"

Ian shot Tucker a questioning look. Folks were highly secretive regarding anything about their prospecting.

Tucker hitched his right shoulder in a motion as if to say, *Who cares?*

"We spent valuable time farming, so we've hauled in stuff to process during the cold weather."

"Hope it pays off for you. Socks has a habit of talking too much. Just the other day, he was jawing about whose claim gave up a lot of color this year. I'm not naming names, but only three claims used gold dust to buy their winter provisions."

"Three." Tucker grimaced.

"Could well be that some got more and just didn't use it to pay the storekeeper." Ian set down a crate. "They're smart if they don't. Socks has the biggest hands God ever made. Socks taking a pinch of dust as payment is the same as someone else taking two."

"Yup." Wily slapped Tucker on the back. "Last time you

went to town, coupla fellows were just coming back from Sitka. Did you notice that they paid Socks with cash?"

Tucker thought for a moment. "You're right. They did."

"They're crazy as loons. They should have bought supplies in Sitka. Anyplace else has to have cheaper prices than Goose Chase."

As the men carried the last of the goods to Ian's cabin, Merry and Abrams reappeared. Abrams trailed after Ian. "That's far too much stuff for one man. You won't have room to turn around in your cabin with all that in there. You bein' my neighbor and all, I reckon I could buy some of it off you. For a good price, of course."

"No." Ian wanted to shoo off the pesky old man.

"Oh, go on ahead," Wily said. "Abrams is your neighbor. And he's said he'd pay you a good price. Of course, you and I will have to split the delivery charge."

"Hold on there just a minute!" Abrams scowled at Wily. "Mind your own business."

"I am. I deliver goods. Everyone pays for that service. Since you just told Rafferty that you'd be willing to deal fairly, that means you'd pay your share of the shipping fee."

"I would not! He was coming this way anyhow. It didn't cost nothing extra for you to cram a little more in that odd boat of yours."

"I'm keeping all of the shipment, so the matter is settled."

"Tucker?" Meredith rested her hand on his arm. "Coffee's ready back at our place."

"Sounds good, Sis."

"Don't mind if I do have a cup." Abrams scurried after Tucker.

"Unless I miss my guess, that old leech already had a cup." Wily shook his head. "Leaves me in a quandary."

"How is that?" Merry asked.

"Don't know whether to hope he strikes it big so he'll cash in and leave, or to hope he never gets more than enough to live on because civilized society won't know what to do with that old skunk."

"He's a character, but he has a good heart."

Wily brushed a kiss on Merry's cheek. "You'd find something nice to say about the devil himself."

As Wily went to get coffee, Merry stayed in the doorway.

Ian fought the urge to go over and claim a kiss, too. Only he'd never steal a kiss, and though he was sure of his feelings, Merry seemed oblivious to his interest. He looked at the bundles, then saw the question in her eyes. "I'm not sure which bundle your gift is in, Merry. I'll be sure to hide it from your twin."

"Thank you. It's nippy. Why don't you come warm up with some coffee?"

"I'll have a cup with dinner. Wily's going to spend the night and fish in the morning. I need to clear some space for him."

Meredith nodded. "Supper will be ready whenever you are. It's nothing special—just rice and beans."

"You're a fine cook, so don't take this the wrong way, but it's not the fare that makes a meal. 'Tis the fellowship. I've yet to eat a meal you've cooked that didn't please me."

Long after she left, Ian basked in the warmth of her smile. He quickly sorted through things and determined where to store each item. Putting the food away was simple and straightforward, with the exception that he hid away the new can of Arbuckle's coffee.

The birthday and Christmas gifts he'd requested for Merry and Tucker fit into a crate. He also slid Merry's Christmas gift for her brother in with them. Two paper-wrapped parcels bore Ma's lovely penmanship: "Do Not Open Until Christmas." Ian carefully slid that full crate beneath his bed.

They'd grown parsley and mustard, and Merry now boasted a good supply of those dried herbs. Ma had sent spices, though. Ian opened the cinnamon and inhaled. The scent evoked myriad memories of family and home.

Ma had sent him a union suit and a handsome blue plaid flannel shirt. Da had tucked in seeds for next year's garden. Braden's contribution—a pair of thick catalogs—came with a teasing note about their being a "housewarming gift" for the outhouse. Ian chuckled with joy when he saw Fiona had sent him popping corn.

Last of all, Maggie had sent a flowery tin. Her note said, "Everyone else was practical. Sometimes the impractical is more essential." Puzzled, he pried open the lid. An exotic blend of chopped-up dried leaves gave off a faintly spicy aroma. Tea. Maggie knew he didn't like tea. In a flash, Ian understood. His sister-in-law had sent this for him to give to Merry.

One by one, he prayed for each member of his family. Each night he did so, but being surrounded by reminders of their thoughtfulness and love made Ian appreciate all the more how blessed he'd been to have such a family.

Someday, Lord, I'd love to wed Merry and start a family with her. Could You bless me with her as my wife?

❧

"Something's burning." Tucker gave Merry a wary look.

She pushed him into Ian's cabin. "You're letting out the heat."

"I'm letting out the smoke." Tucker waved his hand in the air. "Ian, are you in here somewhere?"

Ian threw back his head and laughed. "Sure and enough, I am. Merry, did your brother ever do school theatricals? He's got a penchant for acting."

"The only thing I have a penchant for is coffee."

Ian pointed toward the stove. "Over there."

Tucker went over, poured himself a cup of coffee, and let out a long, loud sigh of bliss.

"For complaining about the smoke," Ian's mouth twisted with wry humor, "you're breathing just fine."

"Coffee makes everything better."

Merry dared to peer down into the small pot on the stove. "What is—no, *was*—that?"

"Oatmeal. I added some berries. The middle part tasted okay, even if the edges got. . .crispy."

Ian's mishap couldn't have happened at a better time. Merry and Tucker had just decided to bargain with Ian—she'd use his stove to cook all of their meals there.

"I put a little water in it. Once the water boils, it'll soften the mess, and I'll be able to scrape it out." Looking utterly pleased with himself, Ian added, "I'm going to use it to bait snares for ptarmigan. Birds like grain and berries."

"So you're going to snare some?" Tucker slurped more coffee. The men started to talk about hunting.

Merry continued to stare at the glop in the pot. "Why bother to snare the poor birds?"

"I thought they'd taste good. Don't they?"

"Nothing that eats this would taste good."

Ian slapped his hand to his chest. "I'm wounded!"

Merry laughed. He'd teased Tucker about having a propensity for theatrics, but Ian often waggled his brows or pasted on ridiculous expressions just because he knew it tickled her. She made a show of looking into the pot and shuddered. "You're lucky you're only wounded. I'd think this might be deadly."

"It's supposed to be deadly—for the ptarmigan."

"If it's like anything else you've cooked, it will be." Tucker gulped the last of his coffee.

Ian gave him a smug look. "You're drinking something I made."

"Why do you think I pray over everything I eat or drink?"

Ian approached Merry and clasped her hand in his. "Lass, you're a wondrous fine cook. Aye, and don't let your brother say otherwise. When he eats something I make, there might well be truth in what he said, but when you've done the cooking—well, the prayers are strictly in thanksgiving."

"Thanksgiving! I'm so glad you brought that up." Delighted to have that segue, Meredith rushed ahead. "We ought to invite Mr. Clemment and Mr. Abrams to join us. If we do, we'd need to use the table you made from your sled. It's the only one big enough to hold a meal for all five of us. And if it's okay with you, I'd like to use your stove to bake."

"I told you the day I brought that home, you're always welcome to use my stove."

"You wouldn't be as liable to burn yourself on the stove, Sis."

"You burned yourself? When? Where!" Ian pored over her hands.

Merry withdrew from his touch. Until now, it had never bothered her to have short nails and chapped hands. Pulling her share of the load rated far above vanity. But suddenly, she felt self-conscious of just how rough her hands had become. "It's nothing. Really."

Tucker snorted. "She burns a finger almost every week. It's impossible to control the flames in a fireplace. A stove's much safer."

"It uses less wood, too. From now on, Meredith Smith, you'll cook on my stove. Had I known this before now, I'd have built a fireplace and given you my stove."

"It's too late now. Temperature's dropping." Tucker glanced to the side to make sure Ian wouldn't see, then he winked at her. "From now on, Meredith will have to cook breakfast here, too."

"I could have breakfast started."

"Whatever you start"—Tucker cracked his knuckles— "would undoubtedly finish me off. The only person in the world who cooks worse than you stares back at me in the mirror."

Ian went to his bed and got down on his knees.

Tucker poured himself another mug of coffee. "Ian's praying he'll never have to eat anything I fix."

Pulling a crate from beneath his bed, Ian declared, "Meredith would take pity on me. She'd never subject me to such suffering. Would you, Merry?"

"Of course not. What are you doing, Ian?"

"Getting something." He lifted the lid to the crate in such a manner as to block her view of the contents. It wasn't right for her to snoop, anyway. Meredith turned her back. She heard Ian mutter something, then the lid slammed shut, and she heard the crate scrape across the floor planks.

"Merry." Ian's voice sounded close.

She turned around and practically bumped into him. "Oh! I'm sor—" She blinked.

"We've established that Tucker and I are no help in the kitchen. I'm trading you this for cooking for Thanksgiving." He held out a stack of folded flour sacks. They were all the same pink floral she'd admired months ago.

"How did you get more?"

"I wrote Ma. She sent these. The top one—Ma slipped in a few whatnots you'll be needing to make a frock for yourself."

"Oh, Ian!"

"Tucker, we've work to do. Finish up your coffee." Ian pressed the gift into her hands, shrugged into his coat, and bolted out the door.

Meredith started to shake. She set the fabric down on the table, and pink thread, ribbon, buttons, and airy white lace tumbled out. Meredith couldn't blink back her tears. Looking at Tucker, she rasped, "I can't go on like this. He deserves to know the truth."

"It's none of his business." Tucker's face darkened. He headed for the door and stopped abruptly. "You gave me your word, Sis. I expect you to keep it."

fourteen

"Days are growing shorter." Ian watched the shadows lengthen at an astonishing rate.

Tucker picked up the pheasant he'd shot. As he straightened, he gave the twine on Ian's shoulder a meaningful look. "Long enough for you to take care of Thanksgiving."

"Buckshot's bound to bring down more than a rifle shell." Three pheasant dangled from the twine. "And face it: Clemment and Abrams will each eat a whole bird. Nothing much to eat except the legs on these, anyway. We needed that one you got."

"I'm not so sure Clemment will eat pheasant." Tucker headed back toward the cabins.

"I've noticed he likes birds. Talks about them every time I see him." Ian didn't mention how he'd seen Clemment biting berries straight off the bramble or how he'd stuffed fists full of twigs into the pockets of his overalls. It didn't seem right, finding amusement in someone else's oddity.

"He's getting mighty peculiar."

Concern shot through Ian. "So it's not just my imagination. Do you think it's safe to have him around Merry?"

"He's harmless. Up here, the long winter's night bends some men's minds. Last year, he came visiting a few times. Merry adores him, and he fancies she's like his daughter. Wasn't 'til the very last of winter that he showed signs of cabin fever. Him already getting bizarre, that's not good."

They paused at the tree line and dressed the birds. As he worked around the sharp spur on the back of a pheasant's

113

leg, Ian cleared his throat. "Tucker, if I've done something to upset Merry, you need to tell me."

"She's fine. Why?"

"I knew she liked that pink material, but she's had it for almost two weeks and hasn't done anything with it." Feeling ridiculous for having blurted out his thoughts, he concentrated on dressing the second pheasant.

Tucker grabbed the last one and worked on it. "You haven't done anything. Well, in a way, you did. You went beyond the agreement we made. Merry would cook on your stove, and we'd have Thanksgiving at your place. Giving her the material—"

Ian snorted. "You got it wrong. She's cooking breakfast in exchange for using my stove. Anyway, I saw straight through that whole act. You and Merry already had made up your minds to strike that deal with me before you left your cabin that morning."

"You sound awful sure of yourself."

"And you're evading the issue. I'm not faulting you, Tucker. If anything, I'm trying to convince you that you're bargaining with the wrong party. You and I need to team up. We're already business partners. We need to figure out ways to help our Merry."

"*Our* Merry?" Tucker stared at him.

Ian didn't hesitate. "Aye, our Merry. Like it or not, I have feelings for the lass. Strong feelings."

"Merry has me."

"I expected you'd say as much. I'd not ever question the fact that the two of you are as close as can be. I don't even challenge that bond. But Merry has a bottomless heart. If I have my way, she'll find room in her heart for me."

"Every single man up here wants Sis as his wife."

"I've seen that firsthand. It riles me. Those men don't think past what they want. Merry deserves a husband who cherishes her."

Tucker picked up his rifle. "We're losing our light. We need to go back."

"I aim to court her."

"You might get everything you aim a gun at, but you don't win a woman just because you want her." Tucker dumped a pheasant on the ground and kept walking.

"I agree." Ian refused to waste the bird. A hunter didn't kill just for fun. He scooped it up and lengthened his stride so he walked abreast of Tucker. "What Meredith wants is more important than what you or I want. If she wants nothing more than my friendship, I'll settle for that. If God blesses me by opening her heart to me, then I'll count myself the luckiest man alive."

Tucker shook his head. "This isn't going to work."

"And why not?"

"Just because you and Sis are thrown together for the winter and bored, you'll mistake companionship for romance. Any little thing she does, you'll interpret as a sign of her affection. You're putting her in an untenable position. Just accept her friendship and be satisfied."

"It's her decision to make, Tucker. Merry is easygoing and adjusts with a cheerful heart. That doesn't cancel out the fact that she's a strong woman with hopes and dreams."

Tucker stopped. "No one knows her better than I do. Yes, she's strong—but Meredith is also fragile. I won't let you break her heart."

"That's the last thing I'd ever want. You and I are in full accord over that. But that's as far as what we want matters. I'm not going to pressure her, and I trust that you won't, either. The decision she ought to make is whether I'm the man God wants her to marry. Don't make this a situation where she has to choose between the twin she adores and the man she loves."

"You're taking a lot for granted."

"No, I'm living in hope." Ian shoved a pheasant at Tucker. "You dropped this. Your sister has grand plans for setting an abundant table. We don't want her disappointed."

"Just because you're my partner, I don't have to like you."

Ian threw back his head and belted out a laugh. "Ah, but you do, Tucker. In spite of yourself, you do."

❧

Merry sat down and shook her head at the mess on the table. "I was afraid Mr. Clemment and Mr. Abrams were going to come to blows over the last of the stuffing."

"For once, I'm siding with Abrams." Outrage rang in her brother's voice. "Clemment crammed half of the rice into his pockets."

"Now, now. He did offer to put it back in the bowl." Ian's eyes twinkled. "And his hands were clean, thanks to Merry."

"Probably the first time either of those old men used soap in a month of Sundays." Tucker headed toward the other room. "Speaking of which, I'll dump the tub."

"I'll do that. Go on over and stoke up the fire in your fireplace."

As the men saw to those tasks, Merry started to stack the plates. She didn't have to scrape them—not a single morsel remained. To her surprise, Tucker came back first.

"Ian's dunking the tub in the river. Don't know if it'll ever come clean."

"The river's starting to freeze over. Go make sure he doesn't fall in."

"I'm going—not because I'll have to fish him out. Because we need more water." He grabbed a pair of buckets and sauntered out.

They returned with the tub half full of water and set the

huge thing directly atop the stove.

"You can't do that. I need to dip water out of the reservoir to do dishes."

"River's probably going to freeze over in the next day or two." Ian looked around. He took a large pot and the pitcher to his washbasin. "Tucker and I decided to go ahead and put by a fair supply of water in advance."

"That's smart, but—" The door shut before she finished.

Though she'd need hot water to wash the dishes, cool water would work well enough to rinse them. Meredith dipped the rinse basin into the galvanized tub and pulled it out. Next she dipped the dish basin in and filled just the bottom. When the men returned, she insisted, "I need you to move that tub. Even a little."

"What's the rush?" Tucker motioned for her to sit down. "We want to fill the buckets from our place, too."

"You'll be glad we did. You know how cranky your brother gets if he has to go without his coffee."

Deciding that she'd have to solve the problem herself, Meredith poured water into two loaf pans and put them in the oven. While waiting for them to heat up, she fiddled about the "kitchen" and straightened the food on the shelves, set the spices back in order, and swept the floor.

Ian and Tucker returned. Ian scowled at the tub. "Where's all the water?"

"I dipped some out so I can do dishes."

He dangled his fingers in the water and wiggled them. "Water's warm. How long 'til it's hot?"

"Not long. She drained half of it." Tucker shot her a disgruntled look.

"We can add the water from the reservoir." Ian scanned the room.

Merry asked, "What do you want?"

"A pot. You've used all of them, haven't you?"

"Thanksgiving dinner takes a lot of dishes." She gestured toward the table.

Tucker poured the water from the pitcher into the washbasin. "Here." He shoved the pitcher at Ian.

"Tucker, tell your sister our bargain."

"Okay. Sis, I wash and he dries."

"What kind of deal is that?"

"A smart one." Ian elbowed Tucker in the ribs. "If he puts the dishes away, you'll never find anything again."

"I—"

"You're getting your birthday present from me two days early." Tucker grinned. "Here." He pulled something from his pocket and handed it to her.

She held the item a little closer to the lamp. "Victoria's English cottage rose glycerin soap. Tucker!" She lifted the beautifully wrapped bar and inhaled deeply. "The fragrance is wonderful. How did you get this?"

"When Wily was here, I asked him to tell Socks to order it."

"Thank you." She wound her arms around her brother. "I love it!"

He squeezed her. "While we do the dishes, you're going to shampoo and soak."

Merry laughed for joy. "That's what the water is all about!"

"We thought to mix water from the reservoir with the buckets so you could rinse your hair." Ian motioned for her to move away from the door to the other room. "It'll take time to heat up more dish water, so you're to soak to your heart's content."

"I put water in loaf pans in the oven to use for the dishes."

"That'll work, but it still doesn't mean you have to rush. Tucker, grab a few candles so she'll have some light."

Ian carried the tub, and Tucker grabbed a pair of candles.

Meredith followed them into the room. Tucker pulled a towel from beneath his shirt. "Happy birthday."

Meredith emerged a long while later. The men had done the dishes and were drinking coffee. "I feel utterly spoiled."

Tucker sniffed. "You smell girly."

"Thanks to my brother." She smiled at him. "This was the best birthday present you could have dreamed up. Why don't you go use the water?"

Tucker looked horrified. "And smell like roses?"

"You can use my Ivory." Ian motioned him toward the stove. "Fill a pitcher from the reservoir and heat up the tub."

While Tucker bathed, Ian scooted a stool over toward the oven. "Sit here and sip some coffee. I'll rub your hair dry."

Reaching up and touching the towel wrapped around her head, Meredith hesitated. "I'll wait 'til I get home."

"It's too cold out for that. Here." He patted the stool. "I didn't mean to offend you. If you feel it's improper for me to help you, then please still take care of yourself. Would you like to borrow my comb?"

"If you don't mind."

He handed her his comb. "Whatever I have, you only need ask."

"You're too generous."

"Nay, lass. Our heavenly Father has faithfully provided for me. 'Tis His generosity I extend whenever I share. Today's Thanksgiving—a day to count our blessings. I've my family who loves me, and I've you and Tucker as my new friends. 'Tisn't just my belly that's full. My heart overflows."

"Mine does, too." Afraid she'd been too forward, Meredith hastened to tack on, "Tucker's, too. This year, we have so much for which to be thankful."

fifteen

"Happy birthday!" Ian shoved his door shut and helped Meredith remove her cape.

"Thank you."

For a fleeting second, Ian allowed himself to brush a spiraled tendril of her hair from her nape. It felt baby soft, a realization that made him smile, seeing as it was her birthday.

"I'm the older one. Sis, scoot over. I'm dying for a cup of coffee."

Meredith poked her twin in the ribs. "Being five minutes older doesn't give you leave to be bossy."

"I'm not bossy." He eased past her and tacked on, "Just surly."

"You hardly even say a word to Ian except for wanting coffee."

The last thing Ian wanted was for her to be put in the center of a tug o' war between him and her brother. He shook her cape and hung it on a peg by the door. "I understand. Tucker knows what he likes."

Tucker paused with the coffeepot in mid air. "I know what I love."

"So go on and have a cup." Ian gently nudged Merry toward the table. "And have a seat. Breakfast is ready."

"You cooked breakfast?"

"Oh no." Tucker consoled himself with a swig of coffee.

"I'd be insulted if your reactions weren't warranted. In the past, some of the things I made were—"

"Burnt offerings." Tucker's voice rated as funereal.

"There are a few things that"—Ian grabbed a pair of

120

pot holders—"I did learn to make. These are one of my favorites, so I hope you like them, too." He opened the oven and took out a heaping plate of buckwheat pancakes.

"Flapjacks!" Tucker scrambled to the table.

"How did you manage flapjacks?" Merry gave him a disbelieving look. "It takes eggs to make them."

"Yep. Two of 'em." Ian grinned. "I brought them back from Goose Chase packed in cornmeal. It's a trick my ma used while on the Oregon Trail. Once I got home, I oiled them."

"Enough talk." Tucker patted the table. "Let's eat."

Ian set down the platter and sat opposite Merry. He'd rather sit beside her, but her brother made a habit of doing so—a point Ian noted with a twinge of irritation. *Lord, this is all in Your hands. Help me to have the right attitude.*

"Whose turn is it to pray?" Merry wondered aloud.

"Actually, it's your brother's, but I'd like to ask a special birthday blessing for the both of you." Ian bowed his head and folded his hands. "Our dear, praised heavenly Father, we come before You to start another day. 'Tis a special one—and I'd ask You to look down on Your daughter Merry and Your son Tucker. You've brought them through the past year, and I ask You to hold them in the hollow of Your hand this next year. Grant them health, happiness, and a closer walk with You. Thank You for the food before us, and know how glad we are to be Your children. In Jesus' name, amen."

"Thank you for that lovely prayer, Ian. Among the blessings God bestowed upon Tucker and me this year, you are at the top of the list."

"That's high praise, indeed. I'm honored." In years past, Ian gladly would have eaten every last buckwheat pancake himself. This morning, he found contentment in eating only two and urging Meredith and Tucker to have more.

Once breakfast ended, he went to his bunk and moved the

pillow. "I have a little gift for each of you. Tucker, here."

"No, have Sis go first."

Merry laughed as he swiped the last bite from her plate. "Tucker is older. He should go first."

"Ma taught me not to argue with ladies." Ian handed Tucker his gift.

"A cribbage board? I haven't played cribbage in years." Tucker's joy dimmed. "But we don't have cards."

"Ah, but we do!" Ian pulled a deck from his shirt pocket with a flourish.

Tucker concentrated on the wooden board and ran his thumbnail over the rows of tiny holes. "Thanks."

"What a wonderful gift!" Merry bumped Tucker's shoulder playfully. "Now you won't have to try to learn to juggle. That"—her eyes twinkled with glee—"is actually Ian's gift to me: that I won't have to dodge the rocks you try to juggle."

"Nay, lass. You've a gift, too." Ian could hardly wait to see her reaction. He scooted the pillow completely out of the way, picked up her present, and walked back to the table. "Here you are."

Her hand flew to her mouth, and she stared at his hand. From behind her fingers, her voice sounded breathless. "Hair ribbons."

"Your hair is your crowning glory, Merry." He set the gift on the table before her. As he did, the ribbons shifted, revealing a pair of hair combs and a card of hairpins beneath the lengths of pink, blue, and white.

"Hairpins! Socks doesn't sell ribbons or hairpins." Her warm hazel eyes sparkled with delight.

"Any why would he?" Ian chuckled. "The man's bald as a shaved egg. I wrote home and told my family all about the two of you. I asked for the ribbons. My sister, Fiona, never can keep track of her hairpins. Half the time, she's searching for them at midday. I can't say for certain whether 'twas she or Ma who sent them along."

"Please give them my thanks." She turned to Tucker. "You knew about this, didn't you? That's why you arranged for me to wash my hair! The way you work together—it is such a joy to see what great partners and friends you've become."

"Tucker, we could spend the whole day jawing around in here, or we could actually go out to work and put some muscle behind that partnership."

"Go out to work? Why don't you work inside today?"

Tucker shook his head. "I can't stand being cooped up. There'll be plenty of days when we can't go out. I'm glad to have breathing room." He stood.

Once they'd left Merry and were out of earshot, Tucker stopped. "What you did—it was nice. But that doesn't change things. You can't buy Meredith's affections."

"I'd be a fool to believe otherwise."

"Why did you let her think I knew what you'd gotten her?"

"I neither agreed nor disagreed. We both want Merry to be happy. Aye, we do. On that we agree. And I credit you with loving her so much that you'd have decided to make our gifts complement one another for her benefit."

Tucker shook his head. "I don't know what it is up here that addles a man's mind. There's Abrams and Clemment, and now you. You're all crazy."

"Abrams is a rascal. Clemment—well, I thought perhaps we ought to discuss him. He's not right in his mind. I worry that he'll not take proper care of himself and be a winter casualty."

"Merry keeps track of things. You can write a note to his family. If she doesn't have an address, she'd wheedle it out of him."

"I'll get word to his family. 'Tis the least we can do for a neighbor."

Tucker started rocking the wood-framed steel mesh rocker cradle as Ian dumped small chunks and gravel into it. He added water, and they winnowed through the stones that were worthless.

"Ian? Does Meredith have your family's address?"

Ian didn't pretend to misunderstand what Tucker meant. "Listen here, Smith. If you think I'll bolt off to my old hometown, you're the one who's showing a bent mind. Like this here, I've sifted through stones and pebbles and gravel. I finally struck gold in the form of the comely hazel eyes of your sister. Aye, and that's enough to make me feel rich as Midas."

Ian dumped the top two levels of unremarkable chips of stone. He stuck his forefinger into the very bottom of the rocker box and brought it back up with a mere breath of gold dust on the tip. "A thimble full of this is an ounce. A refiner's fire burns off the dross and leaves it pure. You and I—we're standing in the furnace, but the Lord has different works to do within our hearts and souls. You can call me crazy, but 'tis commitment—commitment to His will and to the woman I love."

"A man who plays with fire gets burned."

"To me, Merry is worth whatever fire I must walk through."

Tucker stopped rocking the box. At the very bottom, only a few flakes glinted. "No matter how much you work at it, you don't always get enough of what you want in the end."

Somewhere, sometime ago, a woman hurt him. Compassion replaced Ian's frustration. "Tucker, whenever a man courts a woman, there's always a danger that things won't work out. I've not pursued anyone 'til now, but that's changed for me. To me, Merry is more than worth the risk."

sixteen

Merry tilted her head and squinted. Ian's bottle window was beautiful to look at but difficult to see through. For the sake of warmth, he'd tacked a hide up over the window and shut the shutters, but for the scant three hours of daylight they had, he'd roll up the hide and open the shutters.

It's so much nicer than last winter. Even a little light is wonderful, and the colors are pretty. They'd gone through a five-day blizzard recently. Being in the small, dark cabin she and Tucker shared felt suffocating. He'd been restless. He'd also muttered about partnerships and not getting enough in the end.

Lord, You know how he worries about the money. If it's Your will to provide enough to cover the debts, we'll be grateful. If You don't want us to be free, then please grant us grace.

She opened her sewing box and pulled out her knitting needles and yarn. For a few hours, she could work on Christmas gifts. Her mind whirled as the yarn played between the needles. *Tucker was upset when we were in our cabin and Ian was over here. He already feels beholden to Ian. Knowing Ian was working here with the rocker cradle while we weren't helping—that has to bother Tucker. I should have realized it before now.*

After finishing several rows, Meredith put away her knitting. She went to the stove and stirred the stew. Mountain sheep, two sizable potatoes, some carrots, and assorted spices mingled to give off a mouth-watering aroma. After filling a jar, she covered the stew once again and put on her russet cloak. She barely touched the door, and the wind blew it wide open.

Snow from the past two days spread before her. Using leather thongs, she strapped on the snowshoes Tucker had made for her. Even with them on, it took effort to walk to where the men were working.

"What are you—"

"Doing out here?" Tucker finished Ian's question. They both looked at her as if she'd taken leave of her senses.

"I'm worried about Mr. Clemment. I'm taking him some stew."

"I'll take it to him." Tucker came toward her with far more ease than Ian did. Merry didn't comment on that fact; Tucker was weaving a pair of snowshoes for Ian as their Christmas gift. They'd be done in time for the worst of the cold months.

"I want to go, too. You can't expect me to stay cooped up all the time."

"Go on ahead." Ian rubbed his gloved hands. "I'll check the snares."

Tucker and she were halfway to Mr. Clemment's claim when Meredith dared to voice what was on her mind. "Ian's cabin has a lot of room. When blizzards hit, if we stayed there, you could work alongside him."

"What's wrong with our cabin?"

"Nothing at all. We made it through last winter just fine. I was thinking more of how he used the rocker cradle and coaxed gold from the silt while you and I did nothing during the last storm."

"I can take a bag of rocks back to our cabin and pan by the firelight."

"Yes, you could. I could, too."

"No, you can't. I'd have to do it over the dishpan so we don't end up with water and ice on the floor."

Meredith said nothing about how Ian had stretched the mountain goat's hide so that it now formed a big, warm rug in his main room. Instead, she said, "We can take turns."

"No," Tucker replied in a harsh tone. "You did all that gardening and earned what we needed for this winter's supplies. I'm doing the prospecting."

"I don't mind, Tucker."

"I do." His voice was colder than the arctic wind.

Mr. Clemment didn't answer their knock. Tucker kicked the door, and it swung inward. The biggest mess Meredith had ever seen stretched before her. Tucker stepped in first, pulled her in, then shut the door. In a low tone, he ordered, "Stay right here. I'll give him the food."

Meredith released the jar and watched her twin shuffle around the mess and toward the table. Mr. Clemment sat cross-legged in the center of the table. He gave Tucker a big smile and gestured grandly. "Home, sweet nest."

"We brought you some chow." Tucker set the jar on the table. When Meredith took a step forward, Tucker motioned her back.

"Food looks good. It'll warm me clean down to my gizzard."

"You enjoy it, old-timer." Tucker came back to her side. "There's not much sun. I need to get Sis back to a warm cabin."

"Off with you, then." Clemment made a shooing motion.

Once he shut the door, Tucker stared at Meredith. "He's not right in the head. Ian and I discussed writing to his family. Do you know if he has any?"

"A brother. I have the address."

"Good. You don't come here alone. Ever."

"You don't want me to get out at all." She sighed. "Honestly, Tucker, I—"

"You're going to listen to me. Clemment was as ordinary as anyone we knew when he first got here. Being here has made him go crazy. You can't trust him for one minute. And like it or not, we're not going to stay with Ian during blizzards.

There's no telling if his mind will snap, too."

ॐ

"A Christmas tree?"

Ian nodded. He could tell how important it was to Meredith. She'd popped out of his cabin, eyes wide with anticipation. "Aye, lass, if you're wanting one, we can do that."

Merry's face lit with glee. "Oh, I do want one!"

"Fine, then. Let me set these inside." He opened the door to his cabin and put down a brace of snow hare he'd snared. Leaving them outside would invite predators.

"Do you want pasties with those, or roast?"

Ian shrugged. "Whatever pleases you."

"I'll let you decide while we choose a tree. I've already crocheted little snowflakes, and we can string cranberries."

"I'm far more liable to eat those cranberries than to string them up."

"You may eat popping corn instead. I don't think we need a big tree. Something about. . .this high."

"Come walk with me. You can choose whichever one you fancy." He'd far rather walk with her alone, but Ian knew Tucker wasn't about to put up with that notion. Instead, he called over, "Tucker! Merry wants a Christmas tree. Why don't you come along and help us find one?"

"There's no room."

Merry smiled. "We can share the one Ian puts in his cabin."

"There's a grand notion." Ian slid her hand into the crook of his arm.

Tucker rested his hands on his hips. "We don't need a tree."

"You're grouchy as a bear." Meredith reached up to pull the hood of her cloak up because it had started to slip.

"I'm not grouchy. I'm hungry."

"Then dress the hare. Ian and I won't take long. Then I'll fry the rabbits, just the way you like them."

Ian steered her off to one side. "I need to fetch my hatchet." He claimed it from just inside the smokehouse. "Now what kind of tree did you have in mind?"

"Pretty. And green and fragrant."

"Any particular variety?"

She hitched her shoulder. "I'll know it when I see it."

They tromped through the snow. Merry made a point of having them walk entirely around each tree so she could make sure it was shaped well and full. Just to prolong their time together, Ian started pointing out flaws.

"You think this one's lopsided?" Merry tilted her head to the side.

"Look at the top. See how the sprigs are veering off?"

"Now that you mention it, they do." She headed toward another one. "The top is pretty on this. I know the bottom has a bald spot, but can't we just chop off the top?"

Ian shook his head. "If we take the tree's life, 'tis only fair the whole of it is used."

Finally they found one that didn't quite reach Meredith's waist. "Oh, it's perfect! Look at it—all around, it's full and green."

Ian had to agree. "It's a beauty. Is this the one you want?"

"Oh yes!"

The crisp air rang with the sound of the ax as he chopped down the little pine. Much to his regret, he still needed to carry the ax and drag the tree, so he couldn't hold Merry's hand.

Bubbling over with enthusiasm, Merry cupped her hands to her mouth and called, "Tucker, we found it!"

"It's about time," he hollered back. "It's getting dark, and I'm half starved."

As they drew nearer to the cabin, Merry's footsteps dragged. Ian figured out what the issue was. "Merry, I'm going to stop a few minutes so I can level off the bottom of the tree. Do you mind standing back a little ways? I don't want any chips to fly up and hit you."

"Okay."

A minute later, Tucker stomped over. "What have you done with my sister?"

"Shh." Ian jutted his jaw toward the outhouse. He raised his voice. "You have to agree, this is a dandy little tree."

"Then my sister picked it out."

"That she did."

"I knew it. You can't sing worth a plug nickel. You can't cook. It was a safe bet you can't find a tree without help."

Meredith reappeared. "You boys behave yourselves."

"Speaking of behaving, I'm going to go check in on Mr. Clemment tomorrow." Ian hastily tacked on, "Alone. He's getting worse by the day. Mr. Clemment probably isn't dangerous, but we're taking no chances."

"We agree." Tucker's words about knocked Ian out of his boots. "Either of us men can stomp over and make sure he's alive. You're not getting near him."

Lord, are we making progress? Is Tucker finally seeing things in a better light?

❧

Meredith could scarcely stand waiting until Christmas supper was over. She'd made gifts for Ian and Tucker—even going so far as to hide them each in sugar sacks so the men wouldn't know what they were. They'd be so surprised!

"Ladies first this time." Tucker went into Ian's other room and came out with a length of wool.

"Tucker! It's beautiful!" She smoothed her hand over the blue, gold, and beige plaid. "So soft and warm."

"Thought you could make a skirt for yourself."

"And it'll give me something to keep me busy. Oh, thank

you!" She smiled. "You even chose colors that match my shirtwaists." Tucker and Ian exchanged a look, and she burst out laughing. "Even if you didn't do it on purpose, it worked out perfectly."

Ian went over and pulled a crate from behind the tree. The strings of popcorn and cranberries danced on the fragrant green needles. "Let's see what we have in here." He lifted the lid.

"Dessert." He lifted out a tin plate.

"Fudge," Merry breathed softly.

Ian chuckled. "Braden's wife and Fiona love Ma's fudge. I'm not certain how Ma managed to sneak any off to us, but here it is."

"The spices and the pink flour sacks and now the fudge— your mother's thoughtfulness. . ." Merry's voice died out as tears prickled behind her eyes.

"Ma's a grand woman. Proverbs 31 says a godly woman's children will rise up and call her blessed. 'Tis easy indeed for me to sing her praises."

Tucker groaned. "Speak them; don't sing them."

Ian chuckled and drew out a handful of pure white candy canes. He hung them on the tree. "We'll save these for another day."

Next he drew out a tin box. "This is from Ma and the girls, for Merry."

Merry blinked in surprise. "But I—"

" 'Tis in keeping with a Rafferty tradition. Each Christmas, everyone receives something practical and something impractical. You'd not want to ruin my Christmas by objecting, would you?"

Merry accepted the tin. "Thank you." She smiled at the beautifully painted scene on the lid. "This is so charming!"

"Did I tell you what Sis did with the paper wrapper on that

soap?" Tucker didn't pause. "She flattened it out and has it pinned to the wall by her bed."

"Did you, now?"

"It's pretty, and so is this." Merry bowed her head and opened the tin and gasped. "Embroidery floss!"

"Doesn't sound all that practical to me," Tucker groused.

"The colors are beautiful." Merry couldn't figure out why Tucker had to be so moody—especially on Christmas.

Bless him, Ian laughed off Tucker's grumpiness. "Lift the paper, lass."

Meredith gently pushed aside the floss and discovered a sheet of paper. A paper of pins, a package of needles, four spools of thread, and dozens of buttons lay below. "I can truly use these. Thank you, Ian." She closed the tin and traced the lid again.

"These are for you, too, Merry." Ian held something out to her.

She looked up. "Skates?" She'd seen pictures of ice skaters, but she'd never actually seen skates.

"With the river frozen, I thought we'd have a lot of fun skating over it." Ian grinned at her. "The surface of the ice is surprisingly smooth."

"It does sound like a lot of fun. Thank you!" She accepted the skates and ran her fingers over the white leather shoe portion. "How did you know what size?"

"He asked me." Tucker's mouth twisted wryly. "It took me three times to check on your old shoes. You kept waking up or turning over."

"I never make things easy on you, do I?"

"Nope."

She beamed at them. "The two of you are incredible. These skates and the material—you've been so thoughtful. I'll remember this Christmas forever!"

Ian returned to the crate and pulled out a brown paper parcel. "Tucker, this is yours."

Tucker tore off the paper. "Netting!" As the netting spilled across Tucker's lap, a thin leather folder fell into view. He opened it. "Hooks and lures. Rafferty, you made a huge mistake. I'm going to ache to fish, not prospect."

"You've brought in many a tasty meal. I'm not complaining about your fishing." Ian reached into the crate yet again. "Tucker, this is for you."

Something jumbled and tumbled inside as Tucker accepted it. "Sounds like a rattler."

"I've never eaten one, but I understand they're edible." Ian tilted his head toward Merry. "I have no doubt that Merry would make it taste fine."

"I wouldn't get near one of those things!"

Tucker lifted the lid.

When he didn't say anything, Merry leaned forward and peeked. "Chess pieces!"

"Do you play?" Ian asked.

"It's been a long time."

Merry dipped her head and ran her forefinger over the metal blade of one of the skates. She didn't want to let out Tucker's secret. He loved to play chess—almost as much as he loved to trick someone into thinking he was a novice. He never wagered on a game. For him, it was a challenge to see how long it took his opponent to realize Tucker knew what he was doing.

Ian said, "We'll have to play a game sometime."

"Sure." Tucker managed to sound offhanded.

To keep from giggling, Merry went to the tree and opened a burlap bag she'd tucked beneath the boughs. She pulled out the smaller sugar sacks and gave each man his. Since Tucker had just opened a gift, Ian went first. He unfurled the blue hat and scarf she'd made for him. He whistled under his breath. "My ears and nose are about to freeze off. This is great! I like blue, too."

"The color of your eyes." As soon as she spoke the words, Meredith realized they probably sounded coy. Embarrassment washed over her. "And—and that nice wool shirt your mother sent."

" 'Tis true." Ian didn't seem the least bit offended. "And the fabric for your skirt that Tucker gave you—the golden stripe in it matches the centers of your eyes." He turned his attention on her twin. "Tucker, what have you there?"

Tucker gave her a funny look. All her life, Merry had been able to read his expressions. Recently, it hadn't always been easy, and on occasion, it was impossible. He opened his sack and drew out a brown hat and scarf. "Real nice, Sis. Thanks."

She smiled and motioned toward the door. Tucker walked over, opened the door a mere crack, and pulled in the gift he'd made for Ian. "These are for you, Rafferty."

"Snowshoes! I've been needing a pair something fierce."

"Yup." Tucker handed them over. "I've gotten cold just watching you wallow in the snow."

"Merry's scarf and hat will keep me warm whilst I learn to walk in these. I've no doubt I'll trip over my own shoes and tumble many a time until I get as good as the both of you are."

"You'll be faster than Sis. She dawdles."

"If you wore skirts"—Merry shook her finger at her brother—"you'd be slower, too."

Ian elbowed Tucker. "You? In a skirt?" He threw back his head and laughed.

"She meant both of us. Didn't you?" Tucker gave her his agree-with-me look.

Merry pretended to sigh. "Actually, either of you would trip on the hems and break your neck if you had to wear all of these layers. Perhaps what I ought to do is use that wool to make myself trousers."

"Over my dead body!" Tucker roared.

"If you were dead, she'd just wear your britches." Ian folded his arms across his chest and surveyed Tucker. "She'd have to hem them up to the knees and take them in a ways, but Merry's a clever lass. She'd wind up with a brand-new skirt and a couple pair of britches to boot!"

"If anything ever happens to me, you're to put Merry on the next ship out. Uncle Darian lives in Seattle. Give me your word on that right now, Rafferty."

"Enough of that talk! You're too ornery for anything to happen to you." Meredith rested her hands on her hips. "And how dare you try to send me to Uncle Darian?"

"He could buy you anything your heart desires."

Scowling at her brother, Meredith demanded, "What kind of woman do you think I am? The things that matter to me can't be bought."

The cabin fell silent.

seventeen

Ian clapped his hands and rubbed them together. "Well, most things that matter cannot be bought. Merry?" He gestured toward the crate.

Excitement replaced her irritation. Meredith half ran to the tree, stooped beside the crate, and rose. "We've saved the best for last. Here, Tucker."

His jaw dropped as she pressed a new Bible into his hands. He cleared his throat, then cleared it again. Emotions flashed across his features. "How?" he rasped.

She'd anticipated his worrying about the cost and had a ready answer. "Ian offered to have his mother shop for me. Things are economical in Oregon, and keeping the secret from you has been fun."

Ian slapped Tucker on the back. "A Bible—now you can't get a more essential gift than that."

"And Ian gave you the chess pieces, so he upheld the Rafferty Christmas tradition—though I have to say, I think having you play chess is practical for me. You'll be too busy with the game to try juggling rocks. I'd rather spend time stitching a sampler than dodging stones."

Tucker held fast to the Bible and cracked a smile.

"While he pores over that," Ian said, "why don't you and I go skate?"

"You have skates?"

He smiled. "My dad sent them to me. They're my impractical gift."

Within minutes, Ian had set several lamps on the bridge.

The bridge always floated just a few feet off the water. Meredith looked at the sight and smiled. "It's hard to remember the bridge is frozen in place. The way the lanterns glow on it makes it look like a shooting star."

"I'd not thought of it that way, but you're right. I noticed instead how they set everything to sparkling—especially your eyes."

Meredith's heart skipped a beat. *Could he be feeling more for me than just brotherly love?*

He chuckled. "Don't be so surprised, Merry. You're a comely lass." He started lacing on his skates. "Fiona always complains 'tis hard to get her skates on tight enough once she's bundled in layers to skate. Braden or I help her. Would you care for some help?"

"Why, yes. Yes, please. Thank you." Meredith couldn't figure him out. He'd complimented her, then compared her to his sister. What did that mean?

A few minutes later, he took her hand in his and helped her step onto the ice. "Ready?"

"I'm not sure. How do I balance on these?"

He gave her an astonished look. "Haven't you ever skated?"

Meredith shook her head.

"You'll do fine. You're always so graceful; it won't be hard at all. Wait here a second and watch my feet. You don't step. Simply glide one foot a little from the front to the side, then the other."

He slid across the ice. "One foot, then the other."

"You make it look easy."

"It is. Here. Hold on to my arm."

Meredith scooted off the bridge and on to her feet. As Ian threaded her hand through the crook of her arm, her legs started to wobble and her feet started to slide. "Oh no!"

"It's okay. I have you."

She clung to him for dear life.

"See? You're doing fine. You're staying upright."

But for how long? She didn't ask.

"Standing is hardest."

"If I can't stand, how can I move? I–I. . .whoa!"

"Here." He transferred her right hand into his right hand and wrapped his left arm about her waist. "How's this?"

Wonderful. Just as quickly as that reply flashed through her mind, Meredith felt her left foot betray her. "I'm like a newborn foal. All wobbly and awkward."

"Not for long."

"Ian?" She held to him in desperation. "If I fall, you'll fall."

"So what? I've fallen hundreds of times."

She jerked away. "That's hardly reassur—ah! Ah! Ohhh!" Her shriek echoed in the air as she tumbled.

Ian sat beside her on the ice. "Not half as bad as you feared, was it?"

"Twice as bad," she whispered.

"Are you hurt, honey?"

Honey. He called me "honey." Warmth rushed through her.

"Merry." He tilted her face up toward his. "Are you hurt?"

She blinked, then ducked her head. "No. Just embarrassed."

His finger tickled her cheek. "It's only me. You don't have a thing to be embarrassed over." He stood and helped her up. "It gets cold down there, doesn't it?"

She nodded and clamped both of her hands around his forearm. "What if the ice isn't thick enough? I could fall and make us crash through."

"A dab of a lass like you?" His laughter rang in the nippy air. "There's no danger of that. Come now."

He made it look so simple. He skated backward and let her hang on to him. Knees and ankles locked, she allowed him to tow her out a ways.

"Merry, you're stiff from the middle clear down to your toes, but the top half of you is bobbing like a washerwoman at the scrub board. Shoulders back. A little more. Yes. Excellent!"

Eventually, she tried to glide her feet the way he did. She plunged down onto the ice and yanked him down along with her. "I'm going to break your neck."

"No, you won't."

Meredith glared at him. "Oh yes, I will. If I live to get off this ice, I'm going to study the Bible and see if there is any situation where murder is condoned."

Ian had the nerve to laugh.

Just about the time Meredith decided to tell him she was an abject failure, she managed eight strokes before stumbling. Amazingly, she didn't fall.

"You're getting a feel for it. You're doing wonderfully."

Just then, Erik Kauffey wandered over. "Well, look at you!"

"Merry Christmas!" Merry and Ian said in unison.

Kauffey motioned toward them. "Same to you. That looks like loads of fun."

"Merry's got natural talent. This is her first time."

Kauffey hooted. "I strapped a pillow to my backside the first few times." He laughed so hard he coughed.

Tucker came out of the cabin. "What's going on?"

"I hoped you'd all be in the Christmas spirit and be willing to trade. I got a plug of tobacco and two peppermint sticks."

"Neither of us uses tobacco." Tucker gave Ian a questioning look.

Ian hitched his shoulder. "Go on ahead and dicker over a cup of coffee, Tucker."

Meredith giggled. "You don't truly think the two of them will have only one cup apiece, do you?"

"It's Christmas. Let them enjoy themselves. I sure am enjoying myself."

"This is sort of fun."

Ian kept praising her. He stayed close and helped her up over and over again. Finally, they managed to skate together halfway around the circle. "We're coming close to the bridge. Do you want to go around one more time?"

Her feet and legs shouted, *No!* But he had his arm around her. Meredith rasped, "Okay. One more time."

"That's my girl!"

Oh, if only I were your girl. That lovely thought kept her going and sustained her almost all the way around. Then a terrible thought struck. *I have no business wanting to be more than a friend to Ian. I'm not really a friend, either. Not a true friend. He has no idea about what happened.*

"Here we go. I'll glide you right next to the bridge. At the last moment, just hold me. I'll spin and slip you right down on the planks."

Moments later, Ian knelt on the ice and unlaced her skates. "How are your feet? Do the skates rub anything?"

"They're comfortable. Truly, they are."

"Good. We'll come skate often." He sat beside her and changed out of his own skates and back into his boots. He tied the laces of the skates together, carried them over his shoulder, and helped her up. "The air is bracing, but as you skate, you stay reasonably warm."

"That's hard to imagine."

"What's hard to imagine is that you've never ice-skated. Now that I think about it, it makes sense. I grew up thinking skating and winter were synonymous. Did you always live in Texas?"

"Most of my life." She didn't want to go into details.

"So tell me more."

She shook her head. "I'm boring, Ian. Nothing about me is worth knowing." *Liar!* Conscience aching, she stammered,

"I'm realizing my clothes are damp. I don't want to catch a chill."

"Go change right away. Better still, go on up to my cabin. I'll go fetch you dry clothes."

"No!"

"But your cabin won't be warm enough."

"I'll bundle up and maybe take a nap. I have a feeling you and Tucker will keep me up late tonight when you start playing chess. You certainly did when you played cribbage!"

"All right. I'll walk you—"

"Nonsense. You need to go change, too."

Later that evening, they ate leftover roast. As a special treat, Meredith watered down a can of Borden's milk and added cocoa. They all sipped hot chocolate and had a piece of fudge.

"You're quiet tonight, lass."

Meredith startled.

"You wore her out skating." Tucker turned toward her. "I'll go on over to Clemment's place tomorrow morning and get the dishes."

"I'm still not sure we should have let Mr. Kauffey drop off the food."

"Clemment's odd, but I don't consider him dangerous." Ian took another sip and hummed appreciatively. "Old Abrams, on the other hand—you get a rifle in his hands, and we'd all better be caught up on our prayers!"

Tucker gave Ian a funny look. "Sis meant that she was afraid Kauffey probably ate the food himself."

"No, no. You're both mistaken. I fear Mr. Kauffey might be taking the ague. His voice was rough, and he was coughing. The thought of him walking any extra distance concerns me."

"The ague?" Tucker shook his head. "It's tobacco. He smokes it whenever he can get some, chews it the rest of the time. That causes a gravelly voice and hacking."

"I've seen that before." Ian unrolled the cloth they'd drawn a checkerboard on. "So, Tucker, are we playing draughts or chess tonight?"

"Draughts. Tomorrow, we can play chess. I want to be well rested. It's a complicated game."

"Aye. Then again, so is cribbage. Once you memorize all the rules, things come quickly."

Tucker gave Ian an assessing look. "You sound like a man who enjoys the game."

Ian gave him a long look. "I don't back away from a challenge."

eighteen

Ian's lantern cast a halo of light into the darkness of the morning. Drops of ice sparkled along the rough, thin fences he'd made of willow branches. Every two yards or so, Ian left a break about the width of his fist in the fence. He grinned in satisfaction that the snare in the next opening held a ptarmigan.

Ptarmigans seemed to prefer the willow branches, and the birds had a habit of dragging their feet in the snow. They'd scurry along the fence and step into one of a series of loops in a length of string. By dragging their feet, they tightened the snare.

Ian set down his lantern and took off his gloves only long enough to take the ptarmigan and reset the snare.

"Well, well." Tucker sounded pleased.

Ian tugged back on his glove, wound the ptarmigan's legs onto the string, and grabbed his lantern. "I'm falling every fifth step," he announced as he lifted one foot. Though he waddled like a drunken sailor on the snowshoes, it beat having to slog through knee- and thigh-deep snow.

Tucker lifted his own lantern higher. "Is that a complaint or a boast?"

"A boast, of course. When first I set out this morning, I fell or stumbled every other step."

"My sister did better than that." Tucker lifted his chin.

Ian didn't take the bait. "I don't doubt that in the least. Merry's a graceful woman. She took to ice skating right off. Aye, she did." Though he'd been facing both of them, Ian

143

focused directly on her. "And I was proud of you for that, lass."

"I have a patient teacher."

"And an impatient brother. I'm hungry, and if Ian didn't start a pot of coffee yet—"

"You needn't bluster. I have a pot on the stove." Ian held out the string of ptarmigan. "We've three of these, Merry. Tucker can dress them whilst I check the rest of the snares. I'm hoping for more."

"I'm drinking my coffee first. I have to wake up. Otherwise, Ian's going to whip me at chess."

"Oh, now." Ian huffed. "The man's going to be making me sorry I brewed that coffee."

Merry laughed. "Listen to the two of you. You sound like boys wanting the first chance on the schoolyard swing."

"Swings are for girls. Tell her, Rafferty. No self-respecting boy wants anything to do with them."

"I'd be lying." Ian paused a second, then added, "Even when I was a mere lad, I always found the lasses fascinating."

Merry didn't bother to muffle her giggle.

Tucker swiped the birds. "You knew what I meant."

"Ian, I can't tell you how thankful I am that you've been so generous about sharing your coffee. Tucker was surly like this once we ran out of coffee last winter."

"You deserve a medal for that." Ian shamelessly took advantage of the opening. "Seeing as I have no medal, I'll take you ice skating this afternoon."

"We're playing chess today." Tucker glowered at him.

"Of course we will. But you promised Merry you'd go pick up the dishes over at Clemment's. I reckoned you'd do that during the light, and she and I can spin around the ice." Ian didn't want to give Tucker a chance to ruin his plan. "I'll be in soon. I just have a few last spots to check."

He walked off. Sound carried exceptionally well on the

icy air, so he heard the Smiths go on into his cabin. "Lord, Tucker's starting to wear on my patience. I don't want things to turn ugly. Could You please open his eyes so he understands I'll not shove him out of Merry's heart and life?"

He reached the last part of his trap line, then returned to the cabin empty-handed. "Sorry I didn't get anything more."

"But these are nice plump ones. I think I'll save the white meat in a bucket of ice for tomorrow and make chicken and dumplings today. That way, Tucker can take something to Mr. Clemment. I worry about him."

Ian nodded. They'd sent a letter to Mr. Clemment's family, but he wasn't even sure if Merry had a correct address for the man's relatives. No one could rely on what the bizarre man said.

Merry plucked a fistful of feathers and added them to her bucket.

"I'll be done here in a minute. Tucker, please stir the Quaker oats."

Tucker complied. "Rafferty, come spring, I want to send a request to your family. I'm hankering after grits."

"Okay. In the meantime, is there someone who might have some? We could arrange a trade."

Both men turned to Meredith. Her brow puckered. "I'm trying to recall where people are from. I doubt Northerners or Westerners would have grits." She named a few possibilities.

Tucker and Ian alternately ruled out each candidate. Most of them lived too far away. With frigid conditions and barely three hours of light, prudence dictated not going any distance.

"I'm more likely to find gold than grits." Tucker sounded downright morose.

"Come spring, we'll turn some of that gold into grits." Meredith set aside the second bird and started on the last.

"Aye, you're right." Ian turned to Tucker. "I suppose that

means you and I had best start working." They went into the adjoining room.

As they'd excavated along the vein of gold, the men had separated out the rocks and gravel that showed promise. Anything that wouldn't bear working, they'd used to make paths between the houses, right by the smokehouse. Come spring, that gravel would keep them all from getting mired down.

The stone they'd chipped out that bore any glimmer of golden hope filled crates and bags in the second room. On the coldest or stormiest days, the men processed the silt in the rocker cradle. On clear days, they'd spread a sheet of canvas outside and use a mallet to pulverize rocks.

"Feels like we're due for more snow."

Tucker nodded. "Guess we'd better bash up some rocks so we can stay busy during the next blizzard."

"We've made faster progress than we anticipated. We're liable to run out of anything to process ere the spring thaw comes."

"It's the rocker cradle." Tucker picked up the canvas and the mallet. "Sure beats standing in icy water with water sloshing over my sleeves."

Ian grimaced. "Wouldn't you know you'd say that? I was thinking that when the thaw comes, gold might wash down-river. I wondered if we'd be smart to devote time to the riverbank, then go back to digging when the ground softens."

"The idea holds merit. If I could do it without having to listen to old Abrams shouting across the water at me, I'd be more inclined to agree."

"He's a character." Ian hefted a sack. They went to the door, set things outside, then returned only long enough to put on their hats, scarves, and gloves.

"The two of you are going to catch pneumonia," Meredith fretted.

Tucker snorted. "Just yesterday, you said I'm too ornery to die."

"We've each a union vest and two wool shirts on. 'Tis sweet of you to worry, but needless."

"It's more dangerous to sweat and ice up than it is to be a little chilly." Tucker threw open the door.

Ian followed him out. Turning to close the door, he gave her a reassuring smile. "We'll not be out long."

They worked steadily, and just as Ian finished pulverizing the last rock, he caught movement out of the corner of his eye. "Abrams is on his way across the bridge."

"Old goat's probably angling for a meal again."

Abrams tottered over. "Reckon dinnertime's here."

"Sundays, after worship, you're always welcome to stay and eat supper with us." Ian stood back as Tucker carefully gathered up the canvas.

"But it's Chrisssmesss."

Tucker stopped fiddling with the canvas and folded his arms across his chest. "I don't let drunks near my sister."

"Awww, Schmith, I only had a few nips. For my rheumatiz."

"That's a few too many."

Abrams pouted like a baby. "Iss your cabin, Ian. Whaddya shay?"

"You don't want Merry to see you like this. It would upset both of you. Go on home."

"But I'm countin' on holiday grub. Mer'dith'll lemme eat. I've been eatin' beans forever."

"You're full of beans, all right," Tucker muttered.

"Thass right. I'm fulla beans. Betcha Merry'll fix me a big ol' roast or ham. Maybe both." Abrams nodded so emphatically he lost his balance.

Ian threw his arm around Abrams. "C'mon. I'll walk you home."

"But I wanna eat. Juss not cat."

"Cat?" Tucker and Ian said in unison.

"Unh-huh. You Bible-thumpers feed folks the fatted cat. Don't want cat. Wanna ham. Thass pig, you know."

"Yes, I know." Ian steered Abrams toward the bridge. "We don't have any ham, but that can't be helped. Next week is New Year's. If you're sober as a judge, we'd be honored to have you over to celebrate."

Abrams squinted up at him. "You're not gonna push me off in that room and make me take a bath in the middle of winter, are you?"

"Let us make a deal about that."

Abrams stopped at his cabin door. "I getta make the deal. If I take a bath, nobody feeds me that fatted cat." He stuck out his hand. "Schake on it."

"We won't feed you cat. Now let me stoke the fire in your fireplace, and you can go to sleep."

From the outside, Abrams's cabin looked small; from the inside, Ian realized he could reach out and touch both sides at the same time. The sight inside would have made Merry's hair stand on end. Items littered the floor, and sacks of staples lay heaped in the corner. A single log burned low in the fireplace. Icicles hung from the ceiling around the edges. To Ian's astonishment, the old man reached up, broke off one of those icicles, and shoved it into a bucket on the hearth.

"Water." Abrams tumbled onto his cot. "I'm schmart. And I don't eat cat."

Ian stoked the fire, added snow to the bucket by the fire, and left the old man to sleep.

❧

Meredith set steaming bowls on the table. "You're right on time for lunch."

"Thanks. It smells great!" Ian peeled off his hat, scarf, and gloves.

She fought the urge to smooth down his riotous hair. The man desperately needed a haircut. Then again, so did her brother. Thanks to the hair combs, pins, and ribbons Ian had given her, she was able to keep her own hair contained into a reasonably ladylike style. *Ian called it my crowning glory. He likes my hair.* That thought made her shiver with delight.

"I invited Abrams over for a New Year's meal, provided he's sober. I hope you don't mind." Ian tacked on, "He agreed to take a bath before the meal."

Laughter tinting her voice, Merry said, "You could have been a politician instead of a prospector!"

"Are the two of you going to yammer the whole day, or can we eat while chow's still warm?"

Meredith sat down next to her twin. "I forgive you for being impatient. It's just that you want to be done here in time to use the light to go to Mr. Clemment's, isn't it?"

Tucker grunted.

After asking the blessing, they ate with very little conversation. Meredith couldn't wait to go ice skating—not because she felt any confidence, but because she wanted to be with Ian again. *He called me "honey" yesterday. And I've caught him looking at me. Can it be that he's developing feelings for me? I hope so. It would be so thrilling to be his wife.*

"Sis? You're not paying any attention. I asked what I'm supposed to take the food to Mr. Clemment in."

"I filled a canning jar. It's over there." She wrinkled her nose. "Please bring back as many dishes of ours as you can find."

"Easier said than done. His place is a mess."

"I know you'll do your best."

Tucker rose. "You haven't been out much. Why don't you

strap on your snowshoes and come with me?"

Heat filled her cheeks.

"Nay. The lass and I already planned to skate. She can go on a visit to Clemment next time."

Tucker yanked on his coat and scarf, then stood by the door.

"Tucker, you forgot the food for Mr. Clemment!" Though the scarf covered her brother's nose and mouth, Meredith could see the ire flash in his eyes. "And take a lantern!"

"I know the way."

"We don't have a lot of light. If you stay awhile—"

"I'm not tromping over there to keep that crazy loon company."

"I don't care how ornery you get—I'm going to match you with my stubbornness."

Tucker let out an impatient growl as he yanked on his hat.

"Give my best to Mr. Clemment." Meredith handed a jar to Tucker. "Tell him to come for New Year's."

"You already told me to do that twice during lunch."

"You're wasting time." She made a shooing motion.

"You're the ones who are wasting time. You haven't taken a hint. I'm not leaving until the two of you are out on the ice."

Mortified that her brother implied they'd do anything improper, Meredith gaped at him.

"The ice is thick." Ian carried his bowl over to the dish basin. "You needn't hold any concern that we'd fall in."

Tucker stood by the door. Ian gave him an opportunity to confess he was worried about their welfare instead of their morals, but he didn't. His silence embarrassed—no, irritated—her. He'd been impossibly grouchy all morning, but this went beyond reason. In a low tone, she demanded, "Apologize for insulting both of us."

Tucker didn't bother to lower his voice. "I won't apologize.

In fact, it would be best if Ian took the food to Clemment."

"Well, he's not. He invited me to go skating, and I accepted. Furthermore, you volunteered to go check on Mr. Clemment. No one's changing the plan. You men are going to play chess tonight." Tucker looked ready to say something, so she cut him off. "I'll just leave the dishes to soak now while we skate."

"I'll help you with your cape." Ian took it from a peg by the door and draped it over her shoulders. As she buttoned it, he shrugged into his own coat.

A minute later, they stood outside. Tucker looked at the skates and lanterns Ian held. "You'd better take those down to the river, then come back for Sis."

She knew he was trying to get rid of Ian. Meredith didn't want to listen to another insult or a lecture about keeping the secret. "Nonsense. I can carry a couple of the lanterns." She grabbed two and started toward the river. Over her shoulder she called, "Tucker, come back in a better mood, or I'm going to hide the coffee."

"That would darken his mood more, Merry."

"It couldn't get any uglier than it is already!"

nineteen

The men exchanged a few words, but the wind whipped them away from Meredith. *I'm an idiot. I should have stayed there. No telling what Tucker is saying to Ian.* Right as she decided to turn back around, from the corner of her eye Meredith spotted her brother walking away.

Ian joined her on the bridge a few minutes later. "I'll set out the lanterns first." He did so, then quickly yanked off his boots and laced on his skates. "Let's have you sit on the edge, like last time." He stood on the ice, took her hand, and helped her sit on the edge of the bridge.

Meredith took a deep breath. "About what my brother implied—"

"I've handled it." He looked into her eyes, then knelt to help her with her skates.

Unable to let the matter drop, she asked, "How?"

He started lacing her right skate. "Your brother's having a bad day. We're all bound to have a few. Even so, I told him I'll not stand for him questioning your honor or my integrity."

"I'm sorry, Ian."

"Nay, lass. Don't be. Tucker loves you. His concern was misguided. He needed to be reminded of a few things. There, now. Hand me your other skate."

Meredith decided not to ask further questions. Tonight when she and Tucker were alone, she could. Maybe when he got back from Mr. Clemment's, he'd have reconsidered and repented. That would clear the air.

"You'll be more confident today once you realize you've

152

learned to balance." Ian helped her onto the ice.

"I'm not so sure of that." She stared downward. "Why are there lines on the ice?"

"I swept it this morning."

"You swept the ice?" She gave him a startled look.

"Aye. Last night's wind carried pine needles and such onto the ice. I didn't want anything to cause you to stumble." He smiled. "And look at you—skating so well."

Her focus shifted. "How did I—ohhh! Ohhh!"

"Here." Ian braced her before she fell. His chest vibrated against her as he chuckled. "You were doing fine until you decided to fret. Let's just have some fun, okay?"

"All right."

Ian stabilized her, but he started holding her hand instead of wrapping his arm around her. When she slid or fell—even when she bowled him down—he never lost patience. "Ian?"

He lay still and propped his head in his gloved palm as if he lay on ice every day. "Yes?"

"How long does it take to get good at this?" She pushed against the ice and sat up.

"To my thinking, you're already doing everything right."

"I fell." She crooked a brow and stared at him. "And I knocked you down. This is the fifth time."

"Sixth, but who's counting?" The corners of his eyes crinkled. "Falling isn't what matters. The important things are if you get back up and if you enjoy yourself."

"I'm having a wonderful time!" She tried to plot a graceful way to get up. "It's the other part that's difficult."

With a lithe move, he got up and extended both hands. "Ah, lass, you don't have to do that alone. Sometimes, 'tis fellowship in the struggle that makes overcoming it all the sweeter."

"As long as you don't mind my struggles." She accepted his help.

He held fast to her hands. Even through their gloves, Meredith felt his warmth. "Mind? Not at all."

"Sis! I thought you were supposed to be skating."

Meredith twisted around. Had Ian not compensated somehow, they both would have fallen again. "Tucker!" She couldn't believe he was back already.

"Sitting around on the ice is idiotic—unless you have a purpose."

"You're not one to talk," Ian called back. "You're lying on the bridge."

"And I have good reason." Tucker took a hammer and struck the ice.

"Tucker!" Terror shot through Meredith. "What are you doing?"

"The ice is too thick for that to cause problems," Ian told her.

"I'm going to fish!" Tucker proceeded to take a saw and cut the hole larger.

All her life, Meredith had loved having a twin. Suddenly, she reconsidered. He had to have run over to Clemment's cabin and back. He was making a pest of himself.

Tonight, when we're alone and under our own roof, I'm going to give him a piece of my mind.

॰

Shouting woke Ian. It took a second for him to realize the source. He immediately yanked on clothes and raced out his door. Tucker never raised his voice to Merry, but he was bellowing at her now.

Ian didn't bother to knock. He plowed straight into their small cabin. Meredith stood close to the fireplace, as if it would stop her shivering. But Ian knew she wasn't quivering from cold.

Tucker scared her.

Irate, Ian turned to Tucker. Tucker paced a few steps back and forth across the cabin. His speech was garbled. He turned to Ian, pointed, and shouted, "Don't know. Go 'way."

Ian stepped toward him. Just as he drew closer, Tucker spun back around. He took two steps, then crumpled to the floor.

twenty

"He's burning up." Ian flopped Tucker into bed and tried to remember what little medical knowledge he'd gathered over the years.

"He's never sick. Never."

The panic in Meredith's voice forced Ian to take charge. "Throw everything you need for a few days onto your bed. I'll carry them to my place and then come back for him. Put on your cape while I'm gone."

There didn't seem to be any rhyme or reason to what Meredith pitched onto her bed. More than anything, they'd need the bedding. Ian gathered up the corners and ordered, "Be quick, Merry. I'll be back in just a minute."

"All right."

He hastened to his cabin, threw another log into the stove, and pulled back the blankets on his own bed. Until that moment, Ian hadn't realized he was barefoot. After yanking on his boots, he went back to the Smith cabin.

"Merry?"

"Come in."

He went straight to Tucker. "I'm going to take him over now. I'll have a better hold if he's not in the blankets. You follow me with them, okay?"

"Okay."

Tucker was limp. Ian told himself that was far better than having to deal with a combatant. Carrying deadweight on a snowy path taxed him, but Ian made every effort to make it look easy so Merry wouldn't have anything more to worry about. She slid past him and opened the door to his cabin. Ian draped Tucker on the bed and turned back to Merry. "I'll put him in a nightshirt. Your cots fold, don't they?"

"Mine does."

"Go back and get it."

Moments later, Ian informed her, "He's got a roaring fever. No rash. That's a good sign."

"What do we do?"

"I have just a few medicinals."

She moistened her lips. "Willow bark is good for fevers."

"Excellent." He cupped her face. "I'll do everything I can, honey."

She nodded, but tears filled her eyes. "That broth powder— I'll make some."

Ian forced a smile. "Only because he's sick. Tucker would far rather have coffee."

Tucker muttered something unintelligible.

ช

"The willow bark isn't working." Meredith's heart twisted as she tried to sponge the heat from her twin's iron-hot skin.

"I'll go see if Abrams has anything."

How long Ian was gone, Meredith didn't know. It felt like forever. A gust of frigid air blasted into the cabin as he returned. She turned with every hope that he'd have a curative. The bleak look on Ian's face chilled her far more than the cold air.

"Clemment's no help at all. Abrams managed to get a good supply of spirits. He's celebrated the holidays and isn't in any shape to make a difference."

Meredith sank down onto the stool and swallowed hard. She reached over and curled her hand around Tucker's. The scar on his thumb he'd gotten from building their cabin still puckered. He squeezed—but so weakly, alarm pulsed through her.

"I'm going to town."

It took a minute for Ian's declaration to sink in. Merry gawked at him. "There's no path. You'll get lost. It's impossible. No one even tries in the winter."

"God will help me." He pulled on the hat she'd knitted him. The scarf, too. Ian came and knelt by the bed. He rested his hand atop hers and Tucker's. "Heavenly Father, You know the concerns of our hearts. You know what Tucker needs. Please, Lord, help us to help him. Keep him in Your hands and give Merry strength and wisdom, and speed me back to them with something that will cure him. In Jesus' name, amen."

Meredith shivered.

"Here, honey." Ian slipped a blanket around her shoulders. He tested her forehead with the backs of his fingers. "You're not sick. That's the best news yet. I'm putting another log in the stove."

"I'll keep trying to get him to take the broth."

"Good."

"Ian? I'm afraid for you to go. And I'm afraid for you not to go."

He looked at her, then said quietly, "We'll make a pact. I'll pray for you and Tucker. You'll pray for me and Tucker. I think he needs our prayers most."

"Okay."

"We'll trust the Lord to make a way." Ian reached for his coat. He yanked it on and fastened it. Hanging from the same peg were his skates. He snatched them. "Merry, God's already made the path."

He left, and she tried to watch through the bottle window as he skated away. Both of the men she loved were in danger.

❧

Ian's hand stung from the cold. He pounded on the doctor's door anyway. He'd not yet met Doc Killbone, but that didn't matter. What did matter was that Tucker's best chance of survival lay with the doctor's knowledge and skill.

Thump, thump, thump. Still no answer.

Finally, the door opened a mere crack. "Doc's sicker'n a dawg. Can't help you none."

"He can still give me advice and medicine." Ian pushed his way past a short, squat man. "Where is he?"

"Asleep."

Ian hollered, "Doc? Doc!"

"He's sick, I tell you."

Ian turned and spotted a gaunt old man in a nightshirt. "Are you Doc Killbone?"

"Yuuuusss." The affirmative sounded as weak and drawn out as possible.

"Tucker Smith's sick. High fever. Nothing's making it break. What do we do?"

"Everybody's sick." Doc rubbed his temple. "I'm outta stuff."

"The mercantile—what does Socks have that would work?"

"No telling what he has." Doc shuffled back toward his bed, but he melted to the floor halfway there. Ian and the man who had answered the door lifted the doc into bed.

Doc closed his eyes and whispered wearily, "Sorry, son. Can't help."

Ian knew beyond a shadow of a doubt that under normal circumstances this man would have come. But these were not normal circumstances.

He went to the mercantile. Instead of going to the front door, Ian went to the back room where Socks lived.

Shoving open the door, Socks groused, "Makin' 'nuff noise to wake the dead."

"Tucker Smith's sick. High fever. What do you have?"

"Not a thing. Everyone else got whatever it is."

Ian refused to accept that answer. "You've got to have something." He brushed past and went into the mercantile. Most of the shelves were empty—but Wily had told Ian that was normal during the winter. Ian lit a candle, whispered a prayer, and scoured the place. Nothing.

"No miracles to be had here. You shoulda had those folks send you medicine instead of all that other junk they shipped."

Heavyhearted, Ian left the mercantile. He walked about ten yards, then jolted. Wily. He was in Skaguay for the winter—but he owned a place here in Goose Chase. He might have something.

Typical of Alaskan practicality, the doors to Wily's home were never locked. Matches and wood sufficient for a fire and food for a meal waited for any desperate wayfarer. Ian bypassed all of that. He rifled through Wily's other possessions.

Please, Lord. Please, Lord. Please. A leather satchel hung from a hook on the back of the door. Tucker grabbed it. The chink and tingle of glass hitting glass made his hopes soar. There, inside the bag, rested four small bottles and half a dozen vials. Each was numbered, and a palm-sized black leather book told what was in each numbered bottle and what its purpose was.

Snow started falling just moments after Ian laced on his skates and started skating up the iced river. With each passing minute, the flurries grew. His muscles tensed and cramped. He wrapped the scarf Merry had made for him over his nose and mouth, but the air was so cold, he felt as if he were inhaling shards of glass. When it became too difficult to see more than a few feet ahead, he kept close to the side of the river. As long as it was on his left, he knew where he was.

Until he fell.

❧

Meredith heard a sound. She hopped up and ran to the door. "Ian!"

He staggered in, and she slammed the door shut.

"You made it!"

He nodded and unlooped a leather strap from around his neck. She shoved him onto a stool and put a mug of coffee into his hands, then took the blanket from her own shoulders and wrapped him in it.

"Everyone. Town. Sick."

"Oh no."

He nodded wearily. "Got medicine bag. Wily's house."

"I was worried sick. This is the worst blizzard I've seen."

Ian's mouth tilted upward. "Bridge. Hit it. Got me home. God was with me."

Meredith set the bag on the table and carefully took out each jar and vial. "Quinine." She read. "Quinine! I know that's for fever!" The tiny book gave the proper dosage. Once she spooned it into Tucker, she turned back to Ian. "Your clothes are soaked. You have to change. Now."

He looked up at her. Though weariness painted every feature, his eyes still twinkled for a moment. "And you called your brother bossy."

Merry kept hopping up to give Ian more coffee and broth. He kept nudging her back onto a stool beside Tucker and draping a blanket over her shoulders. They took turns drizzling fluid into her brother.

"Merry, it's not going to do Tucker any good for both of us to be exhausted. We'll take turns. You lie down awhile."

She gave him a puzzled look.

Ian led her over closer to the stove. The heat radiating there felt so good. He'd set up her cot and had blankets waiting. "Lie down. I'll wake you if I need to."

"Are you sure?"

"Absolutely."

She lay down, but rest wouldn't come. Guilt mounted. Finally, Merry threw off the covers.

"It's my fault. Him being sick. It's my fault. We've always had each other. I made a promise to him. I've been begging him for months now, but he wouldn't release me from my word. I told him that I couldn't keep it anymore. It's anger. That's what this is. It's burning him hollow on the inside. He's mad that I was going to choose you over him. I am all he has, and I was going to betray him. He told me to go ahead and tell you. He told me I could, and he meant it, but look what it's doing. It's killing him. Now he's going to die, and you'll never trust me."

"Merry, honey, he's going to get better. I have faith he is. Aye, I think he's feeling a bit cooler. And he's not restless like he was."

"I didn't lie, but I did. Because I didn't tell you stuff I should have. I'm ashamed. I was living a lie because I didn't tell you something."

"But was it something I needed to be told?"

"Women are supposed to know about healing and stuff. I never learned it. Mama had a doctor, and once she went to her eternal rest, we were so healthy we never needed any help. What if he's not getting better? What if—"

"You're exhausted. 'Tis your fears talking, not your faith. Why don't you rest? It does no good for us both to stay up. If there's something you want to tell me later when things are back to normal, you can."

"You're being noble. That makes me feel even worse. The conviction I carry in my heart tells me it's just as wrong to withhold information as it is to give false information. You've asked about my family, and I've evaded telling you the truth."

"You don't have to tell me anything you don't want to."

"But I want to tell you!"

"But Tucker doesn't want me to know it?"

"I've reasoned with him. He didn't do anything wrong. Our father did. Only Tucker feels our family's honor is gone." She leaned closer. "Father swindled a lot of people back home. They'd just recovered from the awful depression, and Father tricked them into trusting him. We once had a spread with prizewinning livestock. Now the bank owns it."

"I'm sorry. It must have been tough to live through giving up your land and livestock."

"It was, but worse, Tucker was engaged to be married. The girl's father called it off."

Ian looked indignant. "There was no call for that. Tucker is an honorable man."

Meredith couldn't seem to stop wringing her hands. "Worst of all, Father. . .c—committed. . ." The word was too hard to speak aloud. "He took his own life. Tucker feels honor bound to repay all of those people what Father swindled from them."

Bowing her head, Meredith added in a hushed voice, "And now we're no better than Father was. We've misled you. We've taken your food. We've even been mining gold on your claim. That's not the way to return the Christian charity you've shown."

Ian clasped both of her hands in his. "Merry, none of that matters to me. I wish I had enough money to pay back those people so Tucker and you could be free of that burden. God holds us accountable for our own actions, but I think you and Tucker are extraordinary. You aren't responsible for paying back the investors."

"You're not mad?"

"The two of you trusted your dad. He wasn't worthy of your trust. Discernment is a gift, but it's also a matter of wisely gathering information. I thank you for feeling you could trust me, but I don't fault Tucker for taking longer."

Tears streaked down her cheeks. "Will he have that time? Will he get better?"

"God willing."

⁂

Tucker's fever broke. Ian fought the urge to whoop with joy. He wouldn't do that—Meredith needed her rest. She'd no more unburdened her soul than she'd fallen fast asleep. How she'd managed to curl up like a kitten on one of those cots amazed him.

Ian filled a small cup with apple cider and lifted Tucker's head. Tucker took a few sips, then stopped. Every few minutes, Ian coaxed him to take more.

Weariness dragged at him. At one point, he decided to hum.

Tucker's left eye opened a mere slit, and he frowned. "Liar."

"Tucker Smith, are you calling me a liar?"

"No singing." His voice sounded as gravelly as the silt they mined.

Ian leaned a mite closer. "I wasn't singing. I was humming. I gave you my word I wouldn't sing, but I never said I wouldn't hum or whistle."

"Ugh. Hum? Thought. . .mosquito."

Ian grinned. "You'd best open your eyes wider. I'm too small to be an Alaskan mosquito."

"No tune. Mosquito."

"You being sick, you just didn't recognize the hymn 'The Solid Rock.'"

The corner of Tucker's mouth twitched. "I'm better. I'd be sick if. . .recognized that tune." Suddenly, Tucker's brow furrowed. "Sis?"

"Sleeping. She's worn out." Ian lifted Tucker's head and tilted a cup to his mouth.

"Cider." Tucker scowled. "Coffee."

"Nay. Water, cider, or stew. Take your pick."

"Picking." Tucker looked over at his sister. "She picked you. Loves you."

"I was hoping so. She's a rare woman. I'm wanting to marry her, you know."

"Maybe not. Our dad—"

"Your father's not here for me to ask, so I'm asking you for her hand."

"But—"

"Tucker, whatever is in the past is done. No one should have to assume the guilt of another's deeds. Christ alone did that. God is the only Judge, and He grants forgiveness freely through His Son. I don't care what your father did. What I care about is you being my friend, and more important, you being my brother-in-law.

"I'll love Merry 'til my dying breath. Now are you going to give me permission to take her as my bride, or am I going to have to force you to drink more water?"

"Coffee, deal."

☙

Meredith woke to the smell of coffee. She sat up on the edge of the cot and cried out, "Tucker!"

"He's too ornery to be sick." Ian stood and stretched.

"He needs hearty food, not coffee. Ian, you come lie down. I'll sit with my brother for a while. Oh, wasn't the Lord good to us?"

Tucker sat on the edge of the bed and groaned. "I feel like someone hit me with a two-by-four."

"That's not possible." Meredith started to ladle up stew.

"There's no milled lumber around here," Ian said.

"But there are the finest cabins in the world," Meredith countered. "Who else has a bottle-glass-stained window?"

"You'll have one soon, Sis."

"How did you get enough bottles?"

He shrugged—but it was a forced action. "I just have a feeling."

The blizzard still howled. "Do you have any feelings about how long we're going to be burrowed in here?"

"What does it matter?" Ian shrugged. "We have chess, draughts, and cribbage."

"Don't forget juggling," Tucker added. "You need to learn how to do that, Ian. I'll teach you."

Meredith burst out laughing.

Tucker turned to Ian. "What's so funny?"

"I heard you still need to perfect your technique."

"I'm up to two stones at the same time."

Ian plastered a solemn look on his face. "Two. I see."

"Yes, and they're matched, so I can't count on the different colors guiding me."

"Why haven't you taught Merry such a valuable skill?"

Tucker shook his head. "No, no. She'd run off with the circus and leave me behind. I can't have that."

"Wait a minute." Meredith approached her brother. "Are you saying you can't allow me to go off with the circus, or are you saying I can't leave you behind?"

"Unh-huh." He slumped back down and closed his eyes.

"You need more sleep." Ian pointed toward her cot.

"I've had more than you have."

He grabbed a few blankets. "I'll make a pallet."

"You can't do that." Meredith tapped her toes on the floor. "This is far too hard."

"Compared to ice, the floor is soft."

In the middle of the night, the blizzard abruptly stopped. Ian sat up and wondered at the odd hush, followed by a strange singing.

Merry lifted her head. "Oh. The Northern Lights!"

"I've got to see this." Ian yanked on his boots and coat.

Merry hurriedly grabbed her cape. They slipped outside and looked up. Green and red waves and flames danced in the sky.

"What makes the noise?"

Merry shrugged. "I don't know. Sometimes it's much softer. Tonight it's loud."

Ian held out his hand. "Let's go look at them from the bridge."

She slid her hand into his and stood out where they'd have a better view. "Breathtaking."

"Yes," Ian agreed.

Light arced upward and swirled. "I'm so glad I came here."

"So am I. It's been every bit the adventure I wanted, and more." He stared upward. "You know, your brother and I figure that the vein we've found probably isn't going to get much larger. It's worth pursuing, but it won't make us rich."

"I already am rich." She gestured upward. "I have a symphony in the sky and my brother is well. We have a Bible and enough to eat and a good friend and neighbor. What more could I ask for?"

Ian stayed silent.

Finally, Merry got up the nerve to look at him.

He was staring straight at her. "I don't know what more you could ask for, but I know there's still something else I'd want. I long to marry the woman I love."

Merry held her breath so long she got a little dizzy.

"Are you going to ask me who she is?"

She shook her head.

Ian rubbed his warm, calloused fingertips down her cold cheek. " 'Tis you, Merry. You've stolen my heart just as surely as I breathe. If the only gold I ever got from Alaska was the gold in the center of your eyes, I'd die a happy man. Will you be my bride?"

"Oh yes, Ian. I don't know exactly when or how, but you stole my heart, too. My mama once told me love is the greatest adventure of all. You're the man I want to share that adventure with."

As they shared their first kiss, God painted the sky with color and sound.

epilogue

"I get to kiss the bride."

Ian gave Abrams a disgruntled look. "Later. Let me marry her first."

"Can't do that. Once she's your wife, she's a married woman. I wouldn't kiss some other man's wife!"

"I saw the ring," Mr. Clemment said. He wore his overalls the right way around for the special occasion. "It's gold." He nodded. "Gold as the first rays of the Alaska dawn."

"It ought to be. I had the ring made from the gold on our own claim." Ian craned his neck to see out his door. "What's keeping them?"

"They're twins," Abrams opined. "Takes 'em twice as long."

The minister shot a strange look at Ian. "You're only marrying one."

"Don't worry; we'll be sure he picks the right one," Mr. Clemment said in an earnest tone.

The minister tugged on Ian's sleeve. "Can you tell them apart?"

"Yes, Parson, I can. Abrams, go get my bride."

Abrams stepped out the door and hollered, "Hey! This man you wanna get hitched to is gettin' itchy. Best you shake a leg."

The parson tugged at his collar. Ian leaned forward. "Seeing my neighbors reminds me that God has an imagination."

"A big one, indeed."

A few moments later, Tucker stopped just outside the threshold. He set down his sister and brushed a kiss on her cheek.

"See? We kiss her before you swap the 'I do's'!" Abrams and

169

Mr. Clemment both raced over and gave her a kiss on the cheek.

With no church for miles around, Merry wanted to get married in front of Ian's stained-glass window. A golden ribbon of sunlight cast a glow through it.

The parson stood in silence.

Merry finally whispered, "What is he waiting for?"

"I'm sure you want your sister to share this joyous occasion." He bobbed his head.

"What sister?"

Ian fought to keep a straight face. "Parson, Tucker is Meredith's twin."

"Yes, yes. Well, I can see how you're able to tell them apart."

Meredith smoothed the front of her pink dress.

"You look beautiful," Ian told her.

She beamed at him, and the brightness of her smile promised a love that would glow for a lifetime.

A Letter To Our Readers

Dear Reader:

In order that we might better contribute to your reading enjoyment, we would appreciate your taking a few minutes to respond to the following questions. We welcome your comments and read each form and letter we receive. When completed, please return to the following:

Fiction Editor
Heartsong Presents
PO Box 719
Uhrichsville, Ohio 44683

1. Did you enjoy reading *Golden Dawn* by Cathy Marie Hake?
   ❑ Very much! I would like to see more books by this author!
   ❑ Moderately. I would have enjoyed it more if

   _____

   _____

   _____

2. Are you a member of **Heartsong Presents**? ❑ Yes ❑ No
   If no, where did you purchase this book? _____

   _____

3. How would you rate, on a scale from 1 (poor) to 5 (superior), the cover design? _____

4. On a scale from 1 (poor) to 10 (superior), please rate the following elements.

   ____ Heroine   ____ Plot
   ____ Hero   ____ Inspirational theme
   ____ Setting   ____ Secondary characters

5. These characters were special because? _____
   _____
   _____

6. How has this book inspired your life? _____
   _____
   _____

7. What settings would you like to see covered in future
   Heartsong Presents books? _____
   _____
   _____

8. What are some inspirational themes you would like to see
   treated in future books? _____
   _____
   _____

9. Would you be interested in reading other **Heartsong
   Presents** titles? ❏ Yes ❏ No

10. Please check your age range:
    ❏ Under 18   ❏ 18-24
    ❏ 25-34   ❏ 35-45
    ❏ 46-55   ❏ Over 55

Name _____

Occupation _____

Address _____

City, State, Zip _____

Heart♥ng

HEARTSONG PRESENTS TITLES AVAILABLE NOW:

(...ring from this page, please remember to include it with the order form.)

Presents